FruitTramp
Kids

Other books by Bobbie Montgomery:

Keeping Daddy Single
Three Blondes in a Honda
Donkey-Cart Kids

To order, call **1-800-765-6955.**

Visit our website at *www.rhpa.org* for information on other Review and Herald products.

Bobbie Montgomery

REVIEW AND HERALD® PUBLISHING ASSOCIATION
HAGERSTOWN, MD 21740

The author assumes full responsibility for the accuracy of all
facts and quotations as cited in this book.

This book was
Edited by Jeannette R. Johnson
Designed by Bill Kirstein
Cover design by GenesisDesign/Bryan Gray
Cover illustration by Kim Justinen
Electronic makeup by Shirley M. Bolivar
Typeset: 11/14 Veljovic Book

PRINTED IN U.S.A.

04 03 02 01 00   5 4 3 2 1

R&H Cataloging Service
Montgomery, Bobbie, 1918-
    Fruit tramp kids.

    1. Title.

        813.54.

ISBN 0-8280-1422-1

Dedication

To my son,
Theodore Montgomery,
who has felt deprived, because he wasn't
a fruit tramp's kid.

Chapter One

Jo woke up suddenly. Hearing voices, she crawled out of her cot and crept close to the edge of the tent and lifted the bottom of the wall enough to peek out. She could see two mean-looking men. She hoped they wouldn't move into the next camp space.

She let the canvas slip from her hand and listened.

"Shorty, he won't go to the police, will he?"

"Naw, there's nothing to worry about, and he can take care of himself."

"Well, he ain't much trouble, but who wants to be saddled with a kid?" the tall redheaded man said.

"That's it! This is a good place to leave him. I never liked him. What's that in your hand?"

"His swim trunks."

"Just give them a heave over there on his bedroll. I don't want nothin' of his around. You know, his mother never looked like a Mexican, but he sure does. Took after his dad. I don't like Mexes. One thing fer sure, he's a fast hop picker. Maybe I'll hunt him up when the hops are ready."

The short man plunked a small sack of potatoes on the table. "There, he won't starve." The men laughed.

"Here he comes."

Jo could see a dark boy coming from one of the outhouses. Would they leave the boy all alone? Would they come back?

She dressed quickly, went outside, and sat down at the table facing the men. She picked up a box of cornflakes and dumped some into a small bowl. She poured milk on the cornflakes and started eating, never taking her eyes from the scene before her. *What was going to happen? Maybe Mom was right about camps.*

She remembered one evening at the farm. Daddy came home and said, "They got the farm and everything on it, and I still owe money. I can't find a job, but I have an idea. We're traveling to the Yakima Valley. How about that, Jo? You're going to be a fruit tramp's kid!"

Jo giggled. "What's a fruit tramp?"

"It's someone who picks fruit," Daddy explained. "They camp where the work is. When the peach crop is over, they move to where they raise apples. You can't tell what we'll be doing."

Mom looked worried. "All kinds of people, good and bad, stay in fruit pickers' camps. We might meet some real bad ones."

Daddy laughed. "People are the same everywhere."

Maybe these are some bad ones, Jo thought, eyeing the men, as the boy sat down at their table.

Shorty said, "We got this job picking apricots up the line, Carlos. Thought you might like to take a snooze while we're gone. There's your bedroll. You'll be all right. We'll see you later."

The boy didn't answer, but watched the men get into an old Chevy and drive away. He squinted his dark eyes and stared into space. Soon he shrugged his shoulders.

When they lived at the farm, Jo never talked to strangers. But here the only kids she met were strangers, and they all acted like friends.

The boy looked her way.

"Hi, come on over," she invited.

He came slowly and sat down on the other side of the table. She said, "I know your name's Carlos. I heard them call you that. My name's Jo, short for Josephine."

Carlos didn't answer. Jo chatted on. "They don't allow kids in the orchard where Mom and Daddy are working. Mom complains about leaving me alone, but Daddy says I'm 11, and that a fruit tramp's kid has to learn to take care of herself. I suppose kids can't go into the orchard where your dad works."

"Shorty's not my dad. They aren't going to work. They're leaving—leaving to get rid of me. I don't care. He's getting meaner all the time. Sometimes he slaps me around."

Jo shuddered. "I heard them talking while you were gone. I thought I had made a mistake—nobody'd do that to a little boy."

She set a bowl of cornflakes in front of Carlos and poured milk over the cereal. "There, eat that. Mom says things don't look so bad if your tummy's full."

Carlos picked up a spoon and started eating. Then he stopped. "I'm not a little boy; I'm 12! And I want you to know I'm lucky they left. Old Shorty never did a nice thing for my mother. When I get older and bigger—especially bigger—I'll fix him."

Jo remembered one of Daddy's mottoes: a stinker sets a trap and walks into it. Carlos should let Shorty walk into his own trap.

Carlos fumed, "Nobody! I don't need nobody!"

Jo asked, "Where's your mother?"

"You're kinda nosey. If you must know, my mother got sick in California and had to go to the hospital. Before she died, she asked Shorty to take care of me, and Shorty said 'Sure.' I heard him. He lied. He was nice when my mother married him. Then he started drinking and getting mean. I guess he always drank, but Mother didn't know it. He threw things and hit her. I'll get him for that."

Being practical, Jo asked, "How long did they pay rent for, one night or a week?"

Carlos snorted. "Pay! They didn't pay! Shorty yelled to the guy at the gas station, 'We'll be back.' Then they dumped me and left."

Jo said, "You can put your things near our camp. Sunday, when the camp boss comes around to collect the rent, he'll think you're with us, if he notices anything."

"Thanks. I'll put 'em behind the tent where your folks can't see. They won't even know I'm here."

Jo frowned. She always told her parents what happened during the day, but this seemed different. Daddy would report Shorty, and the police would make him come after Carlos. Shorty would be mad and beat Carlos up for sure. She decided to keep it a secret.

She said, "Carlos, let's wait to make your camp. That woman with the crazy boys is watching us."

"What woman?"

"Over by the water faucet."

"H'mmm, I want a drink. Want to walk around camp?"

Jo said, "OK."

They crossed the empty camp space to the water

faucet and leaned way over a puddle of water to get their drinks.

Jo said, "See?" She nodded her head toward two long ropes tied to a truck bumper with the other ends wrapped around the waists of two young men. The men had black hair and dark shaggy eyebrows. Their bib overalls and red plaid shirts looked too big for them. Jo shivered when they stared with their mouths hanging loose. Both of them stuck out their hands. "Candy, candy," they begged.

A woman with gray hair and an angry look on her face stood in the doorway of a large, heavy green tent. "Now you two go on. These are good boys. They won't hurt you. Don't hang around here."

"Don't worry," Jo muttered, as they went down the camp road.

Carlos shrugged his shoulders.

Jo said, "I asked Daddy if those men were wild. I thought they might get loose. Daddy said, 'No, they aren't wild. She has them tied so they won't get hurt or lost, wandering around. There's something wrong with their brains.'"

"It's not their fault," Carlos said. "But I guess they make her crabby. Crabs are always nosey."

Mitsy, Jo's little white terrier, followed Jo closely and sniffed often at Carlos. "I guess she'll get used to me pretty soon," Carlos said, and stooped over to pet her. She wagged her stubby tail, hesitantly at first, but soon was walking between the two of them.

They went by a camp where five kids sat on the grass in front of their tent. The oldest girl yelled at first one, and then another, reminding them that she was boss and their dad would lick them if they didn't mind her. A little girl came running from the outhouse yelling.

"Shut up!" the big girl screamed back at her.

Jo said, "Let's hurry. They're mean to each other."

"They were at Marysville, in the peaches, last year," Carlos explained. "Their dad's always spanking them for nothing. He's got spankiotus from worrying about how to support his big family."

Jo laughed. "Is spankiotus catching?"

"No," Carlos grinned.

They came to the fence and circled back toward Jo's camp. Suddenly Carlos exclaimed, "Hey, somebody broke camp. Let's poke around."

Jo found a wooden box. She said, "You'll need this for your things."

Carlos grabbed a gallon pail from the ground. "Yeah, and I can carry water in this."

"Carlos, you really need a dish and spoon too."

Carlos interrupted, "I don't know what for. Especially after the spuds are gone. I'll have to eat them raw!" He laughed.

"I'll share," Jo promised.

"You can't do that. Sharing costs money; besides, your folks'd catch on."

Jo thought to herself, *What's he going to do for food? Of course, I'll share.*

Nearing the entrance of the camp, Jo glanced at the gas station and store. Outside, an old couple sat on worn car seats, pushed against the wall. The man got up as a customer stopped for gas. The woman fumbled in her apron pocket and popped something into her mouth.

When they came to her camp, Jo said, "That nosey woman isn't around to watch. Hurry with your things."

They spread Carlos's bed on the ground among the young cottonwood trees behind Jo's tent. Carlos arranged the box by his bed and put his extra clothes in it. She noticed how Carlos carefully hid a large leather envelope between his clothes. She supposed he had special things in it. He pulled his toothbrush and jackknife out of his pocket and laid them on top. "Shorty's got my toothpaste. He won't use it. He and my mother had an awful fight about his smelly mouth."

Jo ran into her tent and brought out a sample tube of toothpaste that she had sent away for. She'd also collected a bar of soap, a washcloth, and a small towel. "Here, Carlos, add this to your box. Your mother would want you to keep clean."

"Thanks! She sure would!"

They wandered over to Jo's camp, and she discovered a brown paper bag on the table with "Surprise" written on it. Jo opened the bag. It had a book inside: *How to Teach Your Dog Tricks.*

"Oh, good! Mom knows I want Mitsy to do tricks."

They spent a long time teaching Mitsy. She caught on quickly. Jo said to Mitsy, "You're doing fine, but you need lots of practice. We'll do it every day."

Before Mom and Daddy came from work, Carlos sneaked around to his hideaway.

Mom and Daddy were tired and covered with white spray from the fruit trees. It took them a long time to heat water and get cleaned up. It was almost dark when they finally had supper. They washed the dishes, and Daddy insisted they go right to bed.

Jo worried about Carlos. She hadn't had a chance to share her food with him. She kept thinking about him eating a raw potato for supper. *You can't get help from your parents if it's a secret,* she mourned.

But a lady who went around to each camp, visiting and giving away little books, had said that God would take care of you if you asked Him to. She thought about that as she went to sleep.

Chapter Two

The next morning, after Jo's folks went to work, she called Carlos to eat breakfast with her. She asked, "Were you awful hungry last night?"

"No. I don't pay attention to my stomach. Shorty didn't give me much to eat anyway."

Jo did the camp chores her mom expected of her and later, when it started getting hot, she said to Carlos, "Let's go swimming. Mom and Daddy found a good place the other day."

"Might as well."

Jo went into the tent to put on her bathing suit. She pulled a long sleeved shirt over her suit and buttoned the cuffs at the wrists. It was a boy's shirt. She had four of them. Mom cut the tails off and hemmed them. She never took her shirt off when swimming, or rolled up her sleeves at any time, for dark brown zig-zaggy spots covered her arms. She hated them, and they embarrassed her.

Carlos ran to the outhouse to slip into his trunks, then left his clothes at his camp.

Jo thought they might need a lunch. She made two huge peanut butter sandwiches and shoved them into a paper bag, along with two red apples.

They went up a small incline and crossed the bridge. Later, they turned off on a narrow gravel road and came to a sandy beach with a few cottonwood trees nearby.

When Mitsy saw the river, crowded with swimmers and people standing around on the riverbank, she kept close to Jo and Carlos.

Carlos commented, "Things'er kinda slack now. Pears aren't ready, and other fruit's finished. Just not much work. That's why they can go swimming."

Jo hid the lunch and their shoes in some bushes. Then they slipped between the parked cars and ran into the water with Mitsy swimming behind them. Jo thought swimming and playing in the water with Carlos was fun.

Carlos swam way out toward the other side. Jo splashed around with Mitsy. Someone stood beside her in the water. She heard a husky voice. "Aren't you going into the deep water with your friend? Are you afraid?"

Jo looked up into the darkest eyes she had ever seen. She decided they were not brown, but black. The young man had dark skin, and the water made his black hair hug his head. He had on red trunks.

"I'm not afraid," she answered. "I can swim, only Daddy says I dog paddle."

"My name is Richard Whitefeather. I have a sister like you, and two brothers a little older."

Jo gazed up and down at Richard Whitefeather. She decided he was a nice Indian.

Mitsy swam to shore and sat down.

Richard said, "Your dog is OK. I'll teach you a better way to swim than dog paddle. Now you swim a little, and I'll give you pointers."

Jo swam a ways, turned, and stood by Richard.

He said, "Number one, don't splash your legs and feet so much. Number two, take long strokes, like this." He swam to show her.

She swam some more, and he made comments to encourage her.

"Better, much better. Now don't forget, and next time we meet, I'll help you more. I must go now." He swam out into the deep water, turned to come back by her, and waded to shore.

Jo said, "Goodbye, Mr. Whitefeather."

He laughed. "Just Richard. I'm not like Watermelon George yet."

"Oh," Jo said, and watched him climb into a shiny black truck and disappear down the road.

Later, she looked around for Mitsy and saw her swimming toward shore. Two boys stood between her and the beach and splashed water in her face.

Jo moaned to herself. "She can't get away. What shall I do?" She sloshed through the water toward the boys as fast as she could and yelled, "Hey, stop that! Leave my dog alone!"

The smaller boy growled and barked like a dog.

Jo yelled again, "Leave her alone!"

The big boy laughed and shoved Mitsy's head under water. Mitsy came up snorting water from her nose and paddling furiously.

Carlos plowed through the water. He came near the boys. "Don't touch her again," he said.

The youngest boy stopped splashing and ran out of the water. The other boy, taller and heavier than Carlos, stood up and challenged, "Try and make me."

Carlos lunged at him. They thrashed around, hitting and punching each other.

Jo ran to Mitsy. She picked her up and held her quivering body close. "Why did they want to hurt you, Mitsy?" she asked. "They could have drowned you."

She looked back at the boys. "They're fighting. He's knocking Carlos down in the water. Mitsy, how can we stop them?"

Suddenly Carlos grabbed the other boy and pulled him down too. Just then someone honked the horn of a truck. The boy jerked away and went to shore yelling, "I'll get you next time!" He climbed into the back of the truck, and the driver drove away.

Carlos came to shore and patted Mitsy on the head. She licked his hand as if thanking him.

Jo and Carlos climbed up the riverbank to eat their lunch. They ate silently, feeding Mitsy bites and petting her. Jo thought, *This is almost like having a brother, and he didn't even ask why I left my shirt on.*

Carlos rubbed the little dog's ears. "Don't feel bad, Mitsy. I'll get him next time. You can bite his heels when he's down."

Jo frowned. Carlos wanted to get even when anything happened. She had feelings like that too, but she tried to ignore them.

"Jo, what's the matter with Mitsy? She's gagging. She can't get her mouth open! Look, she's working her jaws back and forth."

Jo laughed. "It's the peanut butter. It sticks to the roof of her mouth. She always does that when I give it to her."

Carlos laughed too. "Oh. I thought she was sick."

They finished eating and decided to go back to camp. On the way, Carlos picked up an old newspaper he saw beside the road. He shook the dust off. "Hey, look. Here's a picture of a soup line a mile long—people waiting for free soup. It's in Chicago."

Jo looked at the picture. Some of the people who stood in line wore expensive clothes, and others looked poor. She read that none of them had money, jobs, or food. The newspaper called this the Great Depression. She knew the Depression caused Daddy to lose the farm.

Carlos dropped the paper, and they went on to camp. When Jo dressed, she thought, *I'm glad my shirt is dry.*

As they sat on the ground in front of Jo's tent to rest, a truck with a small house built on the back drove into the camp space next to Jo's. Three boys piled out of the little house and helped their folks set up a tent and camp outfit.

The big boy glanced at Jo and Carlos. He came bounding over and gave Carlos a friendly shove. "Hi! Knew you right away from the lettuce in Arizona."

Carlos exclaimed, "John!" and stood up. The two younger boys joined them. Carlos poked one in the stomach. "Hi, Jerry." Then he turned to the youngest one. "Hey, Jim! You been eatin' any lettuce lately?"

They all laughed.

John asked Jo where she was from. At her reply, he said, "You haven't been fruit tramps long. You'll learn to dodge the big machine out there."

Jo puzzled over his remark and decided he merely talked fruit tramp stuff.

She smiled to herself. *I have four friends here.* She felt sad though. Fruit tramps move on. She'd met Dort at the last place they camped. (Her real name was Dorothy.) She thought she had a best friend, but one morning Dort's tent and everything had disappeared. She told Mom the only thing Dort left was an empty space.

Mom said, "There's going to be an empty space under this willow. Daddy found us a job up the line." Mom spoke the truth. In an hour they had the Ford loaded and started on their way to this camp. If she had a brother, she would always have somebody to play with. But she had these friends for a while.

Jo perked up at what John said next. "Carlos, remember Dort? They drove in right after us. They're camped over by the cabins. Let's go see 'em."

Jo screamed, "Dort?" Could it be *her* Dort?

They ran across the dirt road. There stood the brown tent that had left the empty space in the other camp. Dort was unpacking dishes and putting them on the table. She saw Jo and ran to meet her. The girls grabbed hands and jumped up and down. Dort's little sister, Tiny, hugged Jo from the back. Mitsy sat up the way Jo had taught her and watched the reunion. Carlos scooped Mitsy up in his arms. "Aw, Mitsy, pay no mind to silly girls," he said.

Dort laughed. "We're best friends, and we'll bump into each other forever."

Dort's mother called her to help. Jo and the boys went back to Jo's camp and sat down on the grass. Carlos told John what had happened since the lettuce work in Arizona, all about his mother, what Shorty had done, and where he camped.

John said, "I'm sorry your mother's gone. Shorty's a rat. You'll be OK. Nobody'll know where you're sleeping. We'll all help."

Jo said to John, "I'm glad you're camped in the space by us. Now that woman with the men tied up can't watch us all the time."

John said, "Oh, are they here? They picked apples in Wenatchee last year."

After a while Dort and Tiny came over. John said, "Hey, we have enough to play ball."

Jo hated baseball, but she went along to an open space, where they marked off bases. Jim had a hard rubber ball. Dort picked up a little board. "Here's a good bat."

Soon a few other kids joined them, and they chose sides. One of the boys called Jo's name first. She smiled and thought, *That never happened before. At school they always chose me last. When these kids find out I can't hit, it will be the same here. At least I can catch.*

John pitched when Jo stood up to bat. He grinned. "You scared of the ball? Just stand up to the plate. I'll pitch 'em easy, and I promise not to hit you."

At school everybody groaned when she picked up the bat. Somebody would grumble, "Here goes another out!" It made her feel good to have John act nice. She smiled, stood closer to the plate, and tried. She even hit a foul and ticked the ball once.

"Better hit it good this time," John warned.

She hit the ball and made it to first. Both sides cheered. She ran to home base before the other side came up to bat.

Jo noticed how the older children encouraged the little kids and gave them time to reach bases.

Later, John's mother yelled loudly, "John, Jerry, Jim! Supper."

That broke up the ball game. Jim, the younger one, muttered, "Probably nothin' but fried potatoes."

John shoved his brother along. "Shut up, Jim! Be glad we got that."

Dort and her little sister each took one of Jo's hands, and they walked around together. Jo felt like giggling and hugging the girls. What fun it was to camp and have friends who showed up! None of their neighbors at the farm had kids her age.

That night, after Mom and Daddy went to sleep, Jo again thought of Carlos without any supper. Supper seemed to be a problem meal. Then she heard a hoarse whisper, "Carlos, here's a bowl of beans."

Jo smiled. It was John. He'd help.

Carlos would be all right if no one found out where he camped. But they might. The visiting lady had said God used people to help others. It was true; John had given Carlos some supper.

Chapter Three

Dort's mother and father started picking prunes across the road from where Jo's parents worked. John's parents rode with friends to work in the opposite direction.

One morning after everyone left for work, Carlos brought his small bag of potatoes with him when he joined Jo for breakfast. He said, "I'm having a spud party today. We'll get the other kids and go up the river. You bring the salt. I have my knife and matches."

They all thought a spud party would be fun and hurried to finish their camp duties. Carlos and Jo took their cereal bowls to the water faucet and rinsed them. The woman who kept her sons tied to a truck yelled from the door of her tent, "You kids get out of the water. Wash your dishes where you're supposed to, or I'll tell the boss."

Carlos muttered, "Bologna!" He gave his bowl another swish and turned the faucet off.

They met the others in front of John's tent and started out. Mitsy trotted along between Carlos and Jo.

John commented, "Not very many people in camp. Most everybody from here has work today."

At the other end of camp, where the road curved, they went around a pile of slab wood, stacked higher than the tents, and crawled under a fence. They followed a trail through high brush, small trees, and a few big cottonwoods.

John called, "Hey kids, I was down here last year. There's wild cherries farther on."

Jo could hardly wait. She liked cherries. Soon Jerry announced, "Here's some cherries." He bent a small scrubby tree over. Each one picked a handful of tiny cherries. Carlos and Jo stuffed their mouths full of them. The others didn't eat, but watched Jo and Carlos, who choked and gasped and tried to swallow.

Everyone laughed at them. John said, "I forgot to tell you, they're chokecherries."

Jo's mouth and throat felt all puckered up. She threw the rest of her cherries away. Carlos laughed at the joke on them, but she felt disappointed.

They hiked on through some thorn-covered brush and down by the river. After following the river's edge, they came to a rocky beach.

"This is a good place," Carlos said. "The fire won't spread here. It's plenty safe. Let's get a bunch of that brush and broken limbs up by the trail. A storm must have knocked them from the trees."

Jo helped pick up brush and limbs. She watched it blaze when Carlos touched the pile with a match. The flames made her face burn, but she liked standing close to the fire anyway. The heat felt good.

Later, when the fire died down to red coals, the boys placed potatoes in them. Jo asked, "Carlos, have you roasted potatoes before?"

"Sure," he replied.

While the potatoes roasted, they waded in the shallow water and splashed each other. John and Jerry made a pool by placing rocks in a high circle. They chased minnows into it, then let them escape.

Dort said, "We should have brought our bathing suits. It looks like a good place to swim toward the other bank."

"Our clothes will dry," John said. He waded out and dove into the water. They all followed and swam around.

Jo stood and let the water slide past her legs. The current tugged on her pant legs. She gave her belt a hitch just to make sure the river didn't steal her jeans.

They swam back and started to stand in the shallow water. Carlos said, "Hey, my pants are heavy. I can't walk."

"I can't either," Jo yelled as she tried to stand up. She hobbled along a few steps and fell on her face in the shallow water. Dort and Carlos laughed and helped her up.

Later Dort's little sister, Tiny, yelled, "I'm hungry!"

In spite of heavy, wet clothes, they made a mad dash out of the water to the fire. They raked potatoes out of the hot coals with small sticks. The potatoes had a hard, thick, black crust. Carlos cracked one on a rock and mealy white potato spilled out. "They're done! Grab 'em."

Jo burned her fingers while cracking a potato open but thought the spud party was fun anyway.

Dort laughed. "Guess what I have?" She produced spoons from her pockets. "Be sure and give them back, washed," she reminded them.

The only comments Jo heard while they ate were "I want another," "Give me the salt," "Good spuds," "Fine idea, Carlos!"

When the potatoes were gone, Carlos and John put the fire out. Everyone washed their spoons and gave them back to Dort.

Jo exclaimed, "I'm dry!"

"So's everyone," Jerry retorted.

Jo glanced toward the trail. "Oh, look at the horses!" she exclaimed.

Dort said, "They belong to Watermelon George. I saw them last year."

Jo wondered who Watermelon George could be. She remembered Richard Whitefeather mentioning him. She thought the horses were beautiful. Their shiny backs, long tails, and bright manes gleamed in the sun. They stood watching the boys approach. The boys talked low to them. They didn't run away, but seemed to want friends.

John grabbed the mane of the black one and gave a leap to get on its back. He got half way on and had to gradually worm himself up the rest of the way. "See, you can guide him this way." He grabbed a handful of mane in each hand and pulled first to one side of the horse's neck, then to the other.

Jerry led the spotted one by the mane to an old log and jumped on. Carlos liked the white mare. He ran, grabbed at its mane, and leapt on. The rest of the horses ran away.

John helped his small brother, Jim, up behind him.

Carlos called, "Come on, Jo." She held back for a minute, frightened. The horses might buck or run away with them, but she couldn't resist the idea of riding the beautiful white mare. She approached quickly for fear they might go without her. Carlos reached down to help her and nearly jerked her arms out of their sockets pulling her up.

Dort stood back, eyeing Jerry's horse. She said, "I'm not gettin' on old Watermelon George's horses. Besides, Tiny's too little. She might get hurt. I'll keep Mitsy here."

Someone yelled, "Yippee!" The horses all ran wildly through the woods, snorting. Jerry was knocked to the ground by a limb as his horse ran away.

Jo clung to Carlos as she bounced up and down on the mare's back. She wished she could stay put like Carlos.

She cried out, "I'm bumping too high. I'm going to fall off. Stop! I want off!"

"Hang tight," Carlos shouted back. "I can't make her stop. I pull back on her mane, but she keeps goin'."

Jo clung to Carlos. Every time she bounced up she thought she wouldn't land on the mare's back again, but she did. They followed behind John to the old dirt road.

"Stop, fools! Get off!"

Jo got a flash of an Indian man standing in the middle of the road as they passed. He had on a blue polka-dot shirt. His legs looked as if they hung down from under his huge stomach. His long braids flipped back and forth, and his cowboy hat wobbled when he shook his fist. He kept yelling in rage, "Stop! Get off!"

Two young Indian men ran out in front of John and stopped his horse.

"Trouble," Carlos said. He pulled the mare to the right and headed back the way they had come.

The Indian man shouted, "Stop!" as they went by him.

Jo kept bouncing. She felt sharp pains in her side as

27

if a knife stabbed her over and over. She screamed as they left the road and a limb whipped her in the face.

"Hold your head close to my back," Carlos ordered. "We're goin' to the river."

Jo didn't think she could stand the pain in her side much longer. The mare ran along the river and pranced through the shallow water. She wouldn't stop.

Carlos kicked the mare and pulled her mane to the left, into deeper water. "Slide off! Fast!" he yelled.

Jo pushed herself to the back and slid off into the water. The mare's tail flapped her face and mouth as it swished through the air.

Carlos shifted around on his stomach and slid off feet first. The mare made big splashes as she ran to shore and disappeared into the woods. Carlos and Jo waded out of the water and sat down. Jo's side soon quit hurting. She said, "Real dumb. Of course, I rode Daddy's horses on the farm, but they didn't run wild like these."

Carlos laughed. "You're OK. We better head back. John'll probably meet us where Dort's waiting. She's the smart one."

As they walked along, the sun poured its afternoon heat down, and their clothes soon dried.

Jo worried to herself, *What if Mom and Daddy find out about this. They will say I broke an important rule: "Never bother or touch anyone else's property."*

A yell behind them pierced the air. "Wait up!"

John and Jim caught up with them.

Carlos asked, "What happened?"

John panted, "The fat one was Watermelon George. He sure told us off. He said, 'I'm going to the camp boss about you kids coming down here and fooling with my horses.' I told him we were sorry, and we'd never ride them again. He just glared at me and said 'Scat!' So we ran."

Jo hoped Watermelon George would change his mind about going to the camp boss. Daddy would be disappointed in her. He expected her to stay out of trouble.

Jerry, Dort, and Tiny were waiting for them. Mitsy ran to Jo. She barked and danced all around while Jo tried to pet her.

"She wanted to follow you, but we held her back," Tiny said.

Dort said, "Jo, your sleeve is torn loose at the shoulder."

Jo grabbed at her dangling sleeve, flaring around her elbow. *Had anyone seen her arm?* she wondered. How could she hold the sleeve up all the way to camp? Dort took a safety pin from her own blouse and handed it to her. She turned so the others couldn't see and pinned the sleeve to the shoulder seam.

"We'd better get back to camp," John urged after telling them what had happened. "Maybe this business will blow over, and maybe it won't."

Quietly, they walked to the fence and crawled under. They continued on the hard dirt road by the camps. Jo didn't look at the tents for new kids or grown-ups. She was too worried about Watermelon George's threat.

A voice called from behind a truck, "Hey, Mex! Where you been? Somebody's been looking for you."

Carlos's body stiffened, his eyes flashed, and his lips clamped together.

Jo saw at once who yelled. It was the boy who had

pushed Mitsy under water. She noticed how angry Carlos became. He probably didn't like being called Mex. She pulled on his arm. "We're in enough trouble, Carlos. Come on."

Carlos hollered, "Later, mongrel!" His body relaxed some as they hurried on, ignoring the mean remarks that followed them.

"Just wait till the next time I catch him away from camp," Carlos muttered.

Jo said, "But Carlos, my dad says any fool can get into trouble. Do you suppose anyone came looking for you?"

As they stopped in front of Jo's camp, Carlos gave Jo a pondering look. "Maybe Shorty."

Jo ran into her tent and quickly changed her shirt. She came out, gave the pin back to Dort and thanked her. Dort was a good friend.

The kids discussed the possibility of Watermelon George going to the camp boss, then they went to their own camps, and Carlos went to his hideaway.

That evening Jo kept quiet during supper. Daddy asked, "What's the matter, honey? Are you getting tired of this old camp? Can't you find anything to do on these long days?"

Jo smiled at Daddy but felt terrible inside. She couldn't tell him about the spud party without telling about the horses. If she told about the horses, she'd have to mention Watermelon George. She couldn't tell about someone looking for Carlos, because Daddy didn't know he slept behind their tent. Right now it seemed as if she couldn't share any of her adventures. She wondered if Carlos would have to go with Shorty.

Chapter Four

The next evening Jo saw a long black car going slowly through camp. Her heart fluttered and almost stopped. The driver was a young Indian man, and Watermelon George sat beside him. They drove by, looking first to one side, then the other, peering at all the camps. Watermelon George's long braids flopped around under his hat.

Jo looked toward the boys' tent. John turned in her direction, raising his eyebrows. She raised hers in an unspoken reply. She thought the men had driven around camp and out to the highway. But no! Here they were again, stopping in front of their camp. Watermelon George rolled out of the car and bounced rather than walked to the middle of the two camps. Dort and her family were all watching.

Watermelon George pointed at John and his brothers, then to her. "Kids been running my horses—been riding them, no reins, nothing. Could get killed. I tell camp boss; he say tell parents."

Mom and Daddy looked at Jo, then at each other, then at Watermelon George. Jo waited and waited for Daddy to say something. He looked at her as if he couldn't believe what the Indian man said. "Jo, did you ride his horses?"

"Fast!" muttered Watermelon George. "She and dark boy didn't stop when I yelled 'Stop!'"

Daddy asked again, "Jo, is this true? Did you ride this man's horse?"

Jo looked down at the ground and bit her lips to keep from crying, but managed a "Yes."

Daddy said, "I assure you, mister, it will never happen again."

Jo heard John's father yell, "Every one of you boys come here." Then he asked, "Did you kids ride this man's horses?"

Jerry said, "I only rode about a second and a limb knocked me off."

"But you tried?"

"Yes."

"Jim?"

"Yes, behind John."

"John?"

"Yes."

"John, I expected you to keep your brothers out of trouble. Don't any of you move. Mister, these boys will be punished, and they will never bother your horses again."

Watermelon George said, "Humph," and went back to his car. He turned his head before getting in. "Better not."

Mom and Daddy got cleaned up, put the supper on the table, and called her. She knew she better eat or she'd be in trouble about that too.

Before going to bed, Daddy said, "Jo, due to the fact we can't trust you, you'd better go to the orchard with us tomorrow."

"But your boss doesn't want kids there."

"You're right—not in the orchard, but you can sit in the car."

"All day?"

"Yes, all day." He turned to Mom. "Do you think that's a good idea?"

Mom looked sad. "It's the only thing to do. Jo, I'll call you in the morning when I'm getting breakfast."

Jo got up in the morning and quickly dressed. It was cold that early. They started working at 7:00. She shivered as she took Mitsy for a walk. *Carlos won't get into trouble because he has no parents,* she thought. *But it's better to be punished. One nice thing, no one asked about the dark boy the Indian mentioned, so Carlos's secret is still safe.*

They traveled 10 miles, then turned onto a gravel road and drove up a small hill by a big white house with a green lawn and beautiful flowers.

Daddy parked under a large tree. "Stay in the car. I don't want any trouble!"

Mom pointed. "There's an outhouse. You may go to it when necessary, and take Mitsy. She will need to go."

Mom and Daddy walked with some other people between two rows of apple trees. Jo watched until they were out of sight. She looked around and saw a tractor, truck, and some spray equipment. She could see only part of the house. She sighed and petted Mitsy, who looked at her as if asking, "What's all this about?" Jo cuddled her close and pulled a blanket that Mom had put in for her up over their heads. She thought about Carlos and the other kids. She thought, *Dort must be glad she didn't get on any of the horses.* She wondered what they were all doing now. She cuddled up closer to Mitsy and dropped off to sleep.

She felt a shake and looked up into Mom's face. She asked, "Is it time to quit?"

"No, honey. It's only 9:30. I've got to go back. I wanted to see if you were all right. Don't put the blanket over your head."

She watched Mom hurry away and disappear through the trees. She felt her chest tighten, and tears rolled down her cheeks. She felt alone, alone in a strange land, like the girl who ran away in a story she read once.

She put her box of things on the seat and colored a picture of boys and girls playing a game. She finished the picture and started reading *Heide*, but she'd read it before many times and decided to read the part about the monkey. She turned the pages until she found the place where the monkey came through the window. It didn't seem very funny now. She put the book back, fastened Mitsy's leash on, and walked slowly to the outhouse so it would take a long time. She stood and watched some insects flying, then stooped and followed some ants with her eyes.

On the way back to the car she saw a lady in the yard by the house. She had on a pretty flowered dress, and her hair was combed in waves. She made Jo think of Mom before they had become fruit tramps. Mom had always looked pretty then. Now she wore jeans and one of Daddy's old shirts to work in, and a man's cap to keep her hair clean.

Jo climbed into the car with Mitsy. She got out a piece of paper and wrote a story. She named it "Then and Now," then changed it to "The Farm, Then Yakima"—

then changed it back again to "Then and Now."

She put the story into her box and after craning her neck around and sighing many times, Mom and Daddy came for lunch.

Daddy spread a canvas under a tree, and Mom put the lunch out. They didn't say much to Jo, but yelled back and forth to some other apple thinners. Mom did show her some strange blunt-looking scissors and explained that when there's a cluster of little green apples growing close together, they cut off all but one so it will have room to grow big and beautiful.

The lunch hour passed quickly. She knew it would take forever for 6:00 to come. It was getting hot. Daddy had said she could sit outside by the car, but not to go anywhere.

After what seemed like 50 hours, the lady from the house walked over to Jo and said, "Hello! I have an idea. My daughter got behind at school last year. Would you like to come over and help her with spelling? You could drill her on some words and give her a test."

Jo answered, "That would be nice, but I can't leave the car. Daddy said not to go anywhere."

"Your daddy won't care when you tell him I asked you to."

Jo thought anything would be better than sitting where she was the rest of the day. She stood and thought some more. *No, I'm not getting in any more trouble.* "Sorry," she said. "I'd better not."

"When my husband comes in, I'll have him ask your father if you may."

Jo said, "All right."

After the lady left, Jo got out her book, *How to Teach Your Dog Tricks*. She had Mitsy practice sitting up. She tried to teach her to dance, but the ground was too bumpy.

A man came walking through the orchard, straight to her. He had his hat pulled over one eye, and Jo thought he walked like he owned the place.

She stood up when he asked, "Are you Jo?"

"Yes. Who are you?"

He laughed. "I'm Doug. My wife had me get permission from your dad to go into the house and work with Amy on her spelling. Your dad said it would be all right, so go on up to the house."

Jo put Mitsy into the car, poured water into her bowl from the water jug, and went to the house.

She soon sat across a small table from Amy with a spelling book, papers, and pencils strewed around. Amy had dark hair and small gray eyes that she squinted to make herself look mean.

Jo could tell Amy didn't want to do spelling. She soon learned that even if Amy had a nice house, wore ironed clothes, and would be in the same grade next year, she couldn't spell and didn't care.

Jo had her write "dictionary" five times and spell it out loud as she wrote it. That's what Miss Jackson had them do last year. Every time Amy looked at her, she glared.

Amy's mother brought them sugar cookies and lemonade. "Eat all you want," she said.

Jo certainly didn't want more than one with Amy acting so disagreeable.

She gave Amy the test. Amy kept asking her what

letter came next and if city began with "c" or "s." Jo said, "I can't tell you. It's a test."

When Jo marked some of the words wrong, Amy slammed her book on the table and pouted. "My brother helps me, even if it's a test."

Jo replied, "Maybe that's why you're having trouble."

Amy's mother came in. "You can leave now, Jo. We're going to town. Put your things away, Amy, and, Jo, would you like to take the rest of the cookies on the plate?"

Jo looked at the cookies. She didn't want them. She felt a boiling inside. She hadn't asked to come here. She didn't like being told to go. She went to the car and sat a short time.

Mom and Daddy came, waving a slip of paper. Daddy said, "The job's finished for a while. We got paid. We're going to camp. You're lucky, young lady, as it's only 4:00."

They drove into camp. Jo jumped out of the car and ran over where all three boys sat at the table. They looked hot, like Mom and Daddy.

"Where's the rest of the kids?" she asked.

"Dort, Tiny, and Carlos went swimming, I suppose. We just got home. A farmer about five miles from here gave Dad a bunch of vegetables and apples. Dad made us walk after them. He could have stopped on the way home from work to pick them up, but on account of old Watermelon George we had to go after them," John explained.

"Of course it wasn't his fault we rode his horses," Jo stated.

"No, we deserved punishment. We're going swimming. Want to go?"

"Sure, if I can."

Daddy laughed. "Go ahead, Jo. Remember, we don't bother other people's property, and come back soon. It's rather late."

"I won't forget."

They saw Dort, Tiny, and Carlos on the other side of the river and swam over to join them. They sat in the sand and told about their day.

John said, "The man who gave us the vegetables acted about like that woman when you helped her girl with spelling. It doesn't matter. Dad said farmers aren't getting much for their produce. It costs a lot to raise stuff. He said they were lucky to have any money left after expenses."

"Could be," Carlos said.

Jo watched an old car in the distance bounce over the rough road. Jerry piped up, "There goes Shorty, Carlos."

They sat still, watching the car disappear down the road.

"What's he doing?" Jo asked.

Carlos shrugged. "Who knows? I'm going to camp a different way. He's up to something, and I'm not helping him."

Chapter Five

The next morning Dort and Tiny came bounding over. Dort said, "Guess what? The boys are gone! A farmer took them to pick his beans. He's going to pay them!" The girls straightened up Jo's camp, and then went over to Dort's and Tiny's to do their jobs.

Dort asked, "Did your wart go away?"

Jo pulled up her right leg and looked at a large wart on her knee. "No, it's still there. Where'd you get that idea about the dishrag?"

"An old lady, who camped by us in California, said to rub a wet dishrag on a wart, bury it at midnight, and the wart would be gone the next day."

Jo made a face. "It's still there, and it's been two days."

"We didn't wait until midnight," Dort puzzled, "and we were too lazy to dig a hole and bury it."

Jo frowned. "I don't see why dropping it down the outhouse hole wouldn't work, and it was dark as midnight."

"Mama looked all over for her dishrag," Tiny said.

The girls snickered and decided to walk around inspecting the camp. Maybe somebody moved out and left something good.

A lady with white hair called to them. "You girls taking an early stroll?"

They laughed. Dort asked, "Aren't you working?"

"No, I tend camp. I don't go to the orchards. The rest got jobs though, even the old man."

"That's good," Dort said, and they walked on.

Jo listened while Dort spoke to anyone who happened to be in camp. She called it "passing the time of day."

They came to a camp where two tents faced each other with a table between them. A skinny grandma sat on one side of the table, holding a fly swatter. Every time she saw a fly, she'd swat it and say, "Gotcha!"

A young woman sat on the other side of the table, sewing on some pink material. The grandma waved her fly swatter toward some boxes and said, "Set a while."

The girls sat down, and the young woman showed them what she was sewing. "It's for my sister. She's going to have a baby."

In a short time they were talking like old friends. Jo told them about her wart. Dort explained how they'd tried the dishrag experiment with no success.

The grandma laughed. "You come by tonight after the men come in from work. My Jess'll get rid of that wart for you. Wait till the moon comes out."

They talked some more, and when they left Jo said, "I'll be back when the moon comes out."

On the other side of the campground the girls found that someone had moved on. Tiny found a penny; Jo found a little tin box with a lid. "It's tin," she said. "It'll be good for Carlos to put his soap in."

They met two older girls, dressed up, wearing high-heeled shoes.

Dort said, "They're talking about boys."

"How do you know?"

"They're giggling and rolling their eyes around."

Jo laughed.

When they came to the gas station, Tiny spent her penny on a lemon sucker. She offered the girls a lick but they refused.

When they were about to their camps, a loud yell pierced the air. "Dort, Jo! Wait up for us!"

Jo turned and watched the boys jump from the back of a truck and run toward them. Even little Jim flashed a fifty-cent piece.

Carlos said, "We're going to buy stuff for lunch. Meet you at your camp, Jo."

The girls hurried to Jo's camp. Jo put out a loaf of bread and some tomatoes. Dort told Tiny to run over to their camp and get the mayonnaise.

The boys soon dropped packages on the table. Dort opened a large package of cheese and cut it into squares. Jo poured milk, and Tiny opened a package of oatmeal cookies.

The boys splashed at the water faucet to get the dirt from their faces and hands. Suddenly the woman who camped by the faucet yelled out, "Playin' in the water again! How many times have I yelled at you kids about that?"

The boys didn't answer but hurried to their lunch. One of them muttered that he wished that woman would get a job.

As they sat around the table the boys discussed their morning work, and Jo told about her wart. "You must all go with me to have my wart taken off." They agreed to go.

Jerry asked, "Who is that coming this way?"

Jo exclaimed, "Carlos, get into my tent. Quick! It's Shorty!"

Carlos was sitting near the tent opening. Without standing, he slid off the bench and into the tent. By the time Shorty walked by, Jo had the tent flaps pulled down.

Shorty frowned and looked all around before continuing his walk through camp.

Jo went inside the tent and sat down on the ground by Carlos. "Maybe Shorty's sorry he left you. Do you suppose he wants to be nice now?"

Carlos fumed. "You can't tell. He never was nice to me. I can't trust him. He and that partner of his hatch up penny ante stuff. Red isn't with him—he must have had an attack. Sometimes he falls over and froth comes from his mouth. Some people are afraid of him."

Dort and Tiny slipped into the tent. Dort explained, "He's circling the camp and stopping to talk when anyone's around. I'm glad that woman by the faucet stayed in her tent."

John spoke from outside. "He's talking to that kid who calls you Mex."

Jerry reported, "He's going on now." They watched quietly, and Shorty finally got into his car and drove away.

"Aw, let's go swimming," Jerry suggested. "He didn't go that way."

Quickly, they put the food away and walked to the river. Jo wondered about Richard Whitefeather. She hadn't seen him since he helped her with her swimming.

When they came back from the river, Carlos went to his hideaway, and the others to their own camps.

Jo grew thoughtful. Carlos needed help. Shorty

might harm him and make him leave. It seemed like having a brother with him living behind her tent. Then Jo's mom and daddy came home, and all the families were getting dinner. Odors of onions, vegetables, and frying meat mingled in the air.

After dinner John's father called, "Hey, Bruce, some guy's going to spout off down at the other end of camp tonight. You goin'?"

"Might as well go see what the man has to say," Jo's daddy answered.

The two men and Dort's father headed toward the back of the campground, and the kids followed. A small group gathered around a dark man in a crumpled suit coat, who waved his arms around and spoke with vehemence. Jo and the others sat on the ground and took turns playing mumbletypeg with John's knife. Jo grew tired of the game and began to listen.

The man said, "If a horse hasn't got any grass in his pasture, and it's lush and green over the fence, he's going to stick his head under the fence and get some of that green stuff. If you get hungry and see bread in the bakery, you got horse sense, ain't you?"

Jo said to John, "What's he talking about?"

"Oh, you know. No jobs, no place to go, some are hungry."

Jo said thoughtfully, "He's crazy. He's trying to tell people to steal. I guess no one taught him right from wrong." Then she looked up in the sky and exclaimed, "Hey, Dort! The moon's out. Let's go!" She stood up and pulled on Daddy's arm. "We're going."

"All right. Don't wander around."

The boys followed the girls, and Jo explained where they were going.

They stopped by the camp where the two tents faced each other. The grandma called, "Jess, here's the little girl with the wart I told you about."

Jo watched the man come out of the tent. He was a big guy with a shiny head. A fringe of fuzzy hair circled his head above his ears. He wore bib overalls that had been washed so many times they looked white.

He sat down and told Jo to sit on a campstool in front of him. He talked to her in a kind, friendly way, asking questions about her friends and family. Finally, he rolled his eyes around and toward the moon and back to Jo. "You seem like a nice little girl. Where's the wart?"

Jo rolled her pant leg up and pointed to the wart on her knee.

He picked up a little sand from the ground and rubbed it around in his hand, all the time looking up at the moon. Then he put the sand on the wart, rubbed it around, whispering and muttering as he watched the moon.

Jo felt strange and quivery, almost afraid. Then the man looked at her and said, "Now girl, you forget all about this wart. When you remember it again, it'll be gone."

The other kids asked him questions. "Was it magic sand?" "Who did you whisper to?" "How did you know the wart would disappear?"

He wouldn't answer. He shook his head and grinned. "That's a secret," he said. "You do as I said, little girl. The wart will be gone."

Jo said, "All right. Thank you."

No one commented as they went to their camps.

Mom called from inside the tent. "Jo, did you feed Mitsy?"

"Yes."

"She isn't here, and I'm going to bed. Get Daddy to help you find her when he comes home."

Jo walked around, calling Mitsy. She heard a loud whisper: "Hey, Jo, she's here."

Jo ran to Carlos's hideaway and got Mitsy, who was curled up on his bed. She ran back with Mitsy in her arms. What if her mom had gone back there searching for Mitsy?

Chapter Six

Mom and Daddy came home from a short job. Daddy said, "Pay day from both jobs. We're going to Toppenish. It's smaller than Yakima. It won't be so crowded."

It took them a long time to heat water on the camp stove and get ready. Mom said Jo went swimming every day. That took the place of a bath.

Mitsy jumped onto the back seat of the car when Mom tied the tent flaps together and Daddy started the Ford. Carlos peeked around the back of the tent. Jo waved at him and wished he could go with them.

Jo decided it must be payday for many people because the streets were jammed with men, women, and children. She bumped into people—or someone bumped into her—every time she took a step.

Daddy said, "I thought it wouldn't be crowded. I was wrong!"

Jo saw groups of Indians standing in doorways and on corners, talking and laughing. Some of them had long braids, and most of the women had shawls over their dresses. She noticed the younger ones dressed in modern clothes.

Young Indian men shoved and squeezed through the crowd, half running and yelling, "Whoopee! We're gonna scalp a bunch of Whites." They were laughing as a car passed on the street. One of them yelled, "Let's take it!" They ran behind the car and sat on the bumper. The car sped up, and they fell off, still laughing.

Jo heard a man say, "The braves are having fun." She stepped to the edge of the sidewalk to see better. When she turned to ask Daddy if the Indian boys were mad at the White people, Daddy wasn't behind her. She looked around. Mom had disappeared too.

I must find them, she thought, but she was jostled and crammed and everyone seemed taller than she was, even the kids. She tried to dodge between a man and woman. The woman said, "I wish kids would quit running through the crowd."

From the curb she could see a small triangular park between the streets. If she could get there, she'd sit and wait. She knew that if you get lost, the best thing to do is to stay in one place until you're found. She looked both ways, and every way there seemed to be as many cars as people. She waited a long time for an opening between cars. Finally it happened, and she dodged between people and dashed across to the park.

She sat down where her folks could see her. Everyone in the park seemed to be Indians. Many of them, men and women, were sitting on the ground. They paid no attention to her. Two men came toward the bench where she sat. They both wore navy blue pants with creases down the middle of the legs. One of them had on a bright blue shirt, and the other wore a red shirt with white polka dots on it. On their heads were straw hats with hard brims.

They sat down. The one in the red shirt sat by her. He looked down at her and she thought, *Dark brown eyes that look black.*

He said, "What are you doing here all by yourself, Jo?"

After a few seconds she recognized him. Of course, men don't look the same in swim trunks as they do in clothes. "Richard Whitefeather, you never came swimming again."

"Jo, I had to help my people. The reservation where I live needed cleaning up. I've been hauling junk away and helping rebuild houses. Some of them only needed slight repairs; others had to have new roofs. My question again: Why are you here alone?"

"I lost my mom and daddy in the crowd. I thought they would see me here."

Richard laughed. "That's true. So you are lost and need to find your parents. They probably think you are at the police station. Let's go see."

Before they crossed the street, Richard said, "Hang on to my arm. The crowd's thinned out. Many are in restaurants or the movies or inside shopping."

They came to a brick building and went inside. Behind a long counter stood two officers, talking to Mom and Daddy.

Daddy turned and hugged Jo. "Young lady, whatever happened to you?"

"I lost you, and my friend brought me here. He's a swimming friend."

Mom and Daddy turned toward her friend.

"This is Richard Whitefeather," she said.

They both shook hands with Richard and thanked him for bringing her to the police station.

One of the officers said, "Good work, Whitefeather. When can we put you on steady?"

They laughed.

Jo and her parents went outside. Daddy said to Mom, "Honey, give me the grocery list, and I'll do the shopping while you get what you want. I'll meet you at the car." Mom handed Daddy the grocery list.

Jo saw two officers coming up the steps, dragging a man who slurred loud words from his mouth. She heard him say, "I had to defend myself."

One of the officers replied, "Of course. You can sleep your grievances off in jail."

Prickles ran up Jo's spine as she took a second look at the man in the middle.

"Come on, girls," Daddy urged. "Another man who's inebriated, that's all." Jo knew he meant the man had been drinking alcohol, and she knew who it was: Shorty!

Mom grabbed Jo's hand. "Come on; we're going to get you a dress for school and some other things."

"Oh, am I going to school?"

Mom laughed. "Jo, did you think fruit tramps' kids didn't go to school? You certainly will!"

They went into a store. It seemed as crowded as the street. A long line of women waited to pay for their purchases. Jo stood, fascinated, as the lady behind a boxed-in platform put a bill and change into a little metal box, pulled a rope, making the box zoom across the ceiling to the balcony, where another woman opened the box and took the money out. Then she put something into the box and zoomed it back—and there was a customer's change?

Mom gave Jo a jerk. "I didn't know stores still used

that operation. Come on, we're going to look at dresses."

Mom found a big round rack of dresses, some of them in Jo's size. Women were grabbing and yanking at dresses and jabbing each other to get ahead.

Mom said, "I might as well get into this. Don't move." She grabbed at dresses, checked the sizes, put them back, and cried "Ouch" when someone stepped on her foot. She finally elbowed her way out of the crowd, holding four dresses.

"These are all a little big, but by school time they will fit. Choose one you like best— and remember, it's for school. Jo noticed Mom held the one with a white background to one side. She knew Mom wanted her to choose a pretty one, but practical too.

She chose a navy blue dress with tiny green, red, and yellow leaves on it. As Mom started to put the others back, a woman grabbed them from her and said, "I might want them."

"We'll get more things for school next time we shop," Mom said. "I believe we should look in Yakima."

After paying for the dress, they fought their way outside. "Remember, the dress is for school. You must not wear it now," Mom said again. "Let's find the car; our shopping is finished."

Jo laughed. This wasn't the usual way they did school shopping.

They drove into camp, parked, and put their purchases away. John's father called, "Hey, come on over!"

Daddy said, "OK," and Mom handed Mitsy's leash to Jo. "She's been couped up in the car a long time. Walk around a little, and then go to bed. The boys aren't up anyway."

Jo almost jumped with glee. This would be her chance to tell Carlos about Shorty. She walked Mitsy, then circled around behind the tent to his hideaway. Mitsy started leaping on Carlos and licking him in the face until he sat up in his bed. Jo pulled Mitsy away and handed Carlos some candy she had saved from her treat. She sat down by him, and while he unwrapped a piece of candy said, "You'll never guess who I saw being dragged between two officers to jail!"

"Ha! Yes, I can."

"Who?"

"Shorty."

"How did you know?"

"He's the only person you know who would be dragged to jail. He probably started drinking, and then started fighting with someone. He's always sleeping off what he calls 'a spree' in jail. He'll be out tomorrow morning after they feed him."

"Are you sure?"

"Jo, it's happened before."

She felt disappointed. She thought Shorty couldn't bother Carlos anymore, but he would.

Carlos said, "I haven't had the last of him. After you left, he drove through camp twice. Why is he hanging around? He dumped me, but now he's looking for me. This is where he left me. It's a wonder he hasn't figured out where my hideaway is."

"That's true."

"Jo? Jo!" Mom called.

"I have to go. Good night."

"Night, Jo."

Chapter Seven

It was Sunday. Jo liked Sundays because the campground swarmed with people. She could see them walking to the store or standing in line to fill their buckets from the camp's water faucets. Mothers washed clothes in galvanized tubs, while men tinkered with their cars. New people drove in, while others drove out. Jo noticed the family with five kids had moved out. She hoped the father got over "spankiotus"!

This Sunday created a problem, though. She had a difficult time giving Carlos his breakfast. She didn't have a chance to take it to him until Daddy got busy on the car, and Mom went over to John's camp to visit with his mother. Then she put a cold fried egg from breakfast between two slices of bread, grabbed an apple, and went into the tent. She crawled under the back and slipped out to Carlos's hideaway, with Mitsy following behind her.

She found Carlos lying on top of his blankets, staring up at the sky. "Here's some food. What are you doing?" she asked and flopped onto the ground.

Carlos frowned. He took the food in one hand and patted Mitsy with the other. "Jo, I'm figurin'. . . I'm figurin' out 50 different ways to get even with Shorty for the way he treated my mother and for dumping me."

52

"Daddy says that's revenge. It's not your job. God takes care of vengeance. Daddy says that if you let it pass, eventually you won't care about getting even. Shorty'll walk into his own trap, if you let him."

"Yeah. Well, the day we had the spud party somebody else told me about a guy in an old Chevy looking for a Mexican kid. I don't have to wonder who it was. He left me, and I'm not going with him again. He better leave me alone."

Jo watched Carlos as he ate. "I've got to think of some way to get along. After hops and apples, everybody'll scatter. I can't mooch off you guys forever. It's not right. I'll pay you back someday. See if I don't."

Jo felt sad when she thought about everybody leaving. She wondered what Carlos would do. "Carlos, don't you have any aunts or uncles or anything like that?"

"I have Aunt Rose. She's my mother's sister. That's another thing old Shorty did. When we left California, he wouldn't tell Aunt Rose where we were going. They're working in the fruit, but I don't know where. They left Marysville for sure—maybe they went to Arizona. 'Course they have five kids of their own, and the last time I saw Aunt Rose she looked awful big again."

Jo frowned. "We'll think of something. Anyway, Daddy is making what he calls his famous mulligan stew. He lets it cook all morning. It has all kinds of vegetables in it. Come by about noon, and I'll give you a bowl of stew. Daddy'll probably offer it to you before I do."

"OK. I'll be there. I'm going to look for pop bottles. Sunday's a good day for that."

Jo heard Mom say, "Jo, where are you?"

Daddy answered, "She went into the tent a while ago."

Jo scooted back under the tent with Mitsy close behind. "What do you want, Mom?" she asked as she came out the front.

"Run to the store and get crackers to go with Daddy's mulligan, please. Why you want to stay in the tent on a morning like this is beyond me!"

Jo came out of the store with the crackers—and stopped short. Right in front of her was Shorty's Chevy. Shorty was talking to the camp boss. She heard him say, "Well, he's run off. I'm tryin' to find him. His mother's about to have fits."

Jo ran home, gave her mother the crackers, and sneaked out back as quickly as possible. Carlos was gone. She couldn't warn him. Slowly, she went around the tent, searching here and there with her eyes. No Carlos!

John called from the steps of their truck, "Hey, Jo, preacher's coming. I see him and his gang unloadin' over at the platform. There'll be preachin', healin', singin', and yellin'. Let's go!"

Jo looked at Mom. Mom said, "Go ahead. I'll keep Mitsy here with me."

Jo and John started toward a large floor, built on a few two-by-fours, without any walls or ceiling. Many things took place on that platform. Sometimes men put on gloves and boxed, others wrestled. Often the campers had talent shows, and everyone participated. They danced there too. During the week kids played on it. Now they would have church there.

On the way to church, Jo told John about seeing Shorty and what she had heard him say to the camp boss. She added, "He beats Carlos."

John said, "Let's see if his car's still there." They went by the gas station. Shorty's Chevy was gone.

"I wish we could find Carlos and warn him," Jo worried. "Shorty's mean."

"Don't worry," John consoled her. "Carlos is on the lookout for Shorty. He told me so yesterday."

Jo sighed. "I hope so. Carlos wants to stay here."

They joined some other people, who stood around the platform watching two men tune their guitars. Three women and another man stood nearby. They began singing songs about Jesus.

Jo had never been to a church like this. They not only sang, they clapped their hands and yelled Hallelujah at every pause. After singing a few songs, one of the men told what a wicked man he had been and how God had saved him. At the end of every sentence, he yelled, "Praise God!" They sang more songs, and then others spoke until everyone in the group had had a turn.

Jo peeked around the woman in front of her as the leader brought a girl to the platform who was shaking all over. He explained, "This girl has a devil in her. We're going to heal her."

Jo knew that only God could heal—men couldn't. She'd learned that when they went to church at the farm.

The women stepped back, and the three prayed together. After the prayer they began shoving the girl back and forth from one man to another. They yelled over and over, "Come out of her! Come out of her!"

Jo watched in horror as the girl's head began to wobble around. Her face looked white, and she had to be held up.

Jo gasped, "Look how frightened she is. Oh, do you

see those two men going to the platform? They live in one of the cabins."

John murmured, "Something's going to happen. They're mad."

One of the men said to the leader, "That'll be enough of that. The girl needs a doctor. Leave her alone or we'll heal *you*, pronto."

The men stopped jerking and shoving the girl. The leader wiped the sweat off his face and said, "There's apparently an evil spirit among us. Of course I can't heal the girl in these circumstances. Go ahead and sing, folks."

Jo enjoyed the visiting lady when she talked about God, but this seemed scary. She said, "Let's go."

John laughed. "OK."

They met Carlos and Jerry on the way back to camp. Carlos held up 50 cents. "I found a lot of bottles, with Jerry's help."

Jo told Carlos about Shorty. She could see the angry look spreading over his face. He grumbled, "Shorty's up to something. Was the other guy with him?"

Jo replied, "I didn't see him."

"Shorty's got meanness planned and thinks he's going to get me to help him—or maybe he wants me to pick hops for him. I can pick more'n him any day. At any rate, he's up to no good. That other guy's probably in jail. They didn't keep Shorty long. Just like I said it would be."

As they approached camp, Daddy called, "Come and get it. The mulligan's ready." Then he turned to John's camp. "Folks, bring your bowls and come over for dinner."

Jo smiled as they stood in line, waiting for Daddy to ladle out the stew. She felt lucky to have a good father instead of one like Shorty. She was glad Carlos came for stew.

She glanced across the way and wondered what had happened to Dort's family. They were gone when she got up. She wished they could have joined them.

The mothers sat on the bench at the table; the men squatted down on their heels; and the kids lolled around on the grass while eating. Everyone enjoyed the mulligan stew, and Jo laughed because Daddy acted so proud of it.

When they were through, John's mother went to their camp. She returned a few minutes later with a huge sack of donuts and passed them around.

Jo wiped sugar off her mouth just as an old Chevy drove up and stopped in front of their camp. Shorty got out and walked over to them. He inquired, "Any of you folks seen a Mexican kid, about 12 years old, hangin' around here?"

"Boy or girl?" John asked.

Shorty frowned darkly. "Boy."

Daddy stood up by Shorty. None of the kids said anything. Mom started to speak, but closed her mouth when Daddy looked at her pointedly. John's mother glanced at Jo's mom. She didn't say anything either.

Jo looked around for Carlos. Where had he gone? When did he leave?

John's father asked, "Is he your boy? You don't look Mexican."

Shorty answered quickly, "I'm not Mexican. His mother's the Mexican. She's worried about the kid."

John's father asked another question. "Does the boy take after you, or his mother?"

Shorty looked angry. "The kid's Mexican for sure. I've seen him around, but I can't catch up with him. I thought I saw him here."

Daddy looked at Jo. She could feel her tummy squeezing up. Would they find where Carlos stayed? Would Daddy care?

Daddy asked, "You say his mother is worried? That's too bad."

"Yeah, you know women. He needs a good lickin', worrying everybody. I know I saw him here."

Daddy said, "There was another boy here, but he's gone now. I'm not sure where he lives."

John interrupted, "Well, that's not the boy you're looking for. This kid's mother is dead."

Shorty's face flushed deep red, and he hastened to his car and drove away.

Jo waited for the questions she was sure would come.

Daddy said, "He's a mean one. I'm not sure a person should help him."

John's father laughed. "I learned to stay out of other people's affairs a long time ago. In fruit trampin' you meet up with some strange situations."

Mom asked, "Where does Carlos live?"

John answered, "His folks don't camp here."

Jo noticed that John avoided telling everything.

Later, Jo curled up in her camp cot and held Mitsy close. She thought about the brother she often pretended to have. Tonight he seemed to look like Carlos. She sighed, "Carlos is a good friend. I hope old Shorty stays away. He better not take Carlos." She fell asleep asking herself, "Should I talk to God about it?"

Chapter Eight

Monday morning Jo dressed in a hurry, opened the tent flap, and peered over at Dort's camp. Everything looked the same. The car was still gone. Where had they gone?

She thought about Shorty. Would he show up again? She decided not to mention him to Carlos. Then they'd have a better day. Jo put two red apples and the corn-flakes and milk out. Soon Carlos appeared, and they sat down together.

Carlos said, "A new camper came in after dark last night. It sounded like they had half a million dogs."

Jo beamed. "I hope they have some girls. That's what this camp needs. Let's walk over and get acquainted."

Carlos laughed. "OK, but I think it'll be girl dogs, if anything. Let's get the boys and go."

They joined John and his brothers while they were still eating breakfast. Jerry scowled at his bowl.

"What's the matter, Jerry?" Jo asked.

John answered for him. "He's grumbling because we had fried potatoes and Kool-Aid for breakfast."

Jerry pouted. "We have them all the time; besides there's nothing to do around here."

Carlos pushed Jerry's shoulder. "Come on! There's a new camp. Let's see what's up."

"H'mmmph, just people."

John said, "Jerry, snap out of it! Let's have some fun."

Carlos asked, "Anybody know where Dort's family went? I see they're still gone."

"No, but I wish they'd come back. I miss Dort," Jo answered.

John and Jerry washed the dishes and put things away. Then John said, "Let's go."

They meandered along the road past several camps and paused by the pile of slab wood. Carlos pointed. "There's the new outfit."

Jo looked in amazement at the truck with a long, box-like cage perched on its bed. It had white boards nailed on the sides within two feet of the top. Small dogs leaped to the top, again and again. Large dogs seemed to be standing on their back legs, their heads close to a screen above the boards. Soon the dogs began to announce them with yipping, low throaty growls, medium barks, and loud mournful howls.

When Jo was wondering why anyone would have so many dogs, a gray-bearded man crawled out of the cab, holding a sandwich in his hand.

Jo covered her ears as a stream of words came from his toothless mouth. She thought, *Someone ought to wash his mouth out with soap.* When it seemed safe, she took her hands from her ears.

"Hello, young'uns! Dogs are all penned up. None of 'em bite anyway. Come on over and watch. I'm turnin' 'em loose for their mornin' run."

Jo wondered if they ought to go near if all the dogs ran loose. She supposed the old man would cuss at the dogs to make them behave. She might as well see what would happen. Mitsy leaned against Jo, quivering with fright. Jo picked her up and held her close.

"My name's Clem," the old man informed them. "Now watch." He opened the back of the pickup. Not one of the dogs jumped until he called out, "Jack!" Then a long-eared hound jumped down. Clem waved his arm toward the woods. "Go out that way." Jack ran under the fence. Clem called, "Nancy, Jedd, and Rodney!" Three more big dogs bounded down from the truck and dashed into the woods.

Clem looked from the woods to the truck, back and forth, as he called each dog's name, it jumped down to follow the others. The last one was small with long hair. She seemed shy and afraid. He lifted her to the ground.

"How many?" Jim asked.

"Twenty-one," Clem answered. "You know the song, 'Twenty-one Children Came to Bless the Old Man's Home in the Wilderness'? I changed 'children' to 'dogs.'" He bent over, slapped his knee, and laughed.

Jo thought Clem's laughter sounded like a cackle.

The children followed Clem under the fence and along the trail. "I'll carry Mitsy," Carlos offered. Jo handed Mitsy to him.

Clem said, "My dogs won't hurt her none. I won't let 'em." So Carlos put Mitsy down, and she followed close to Jo's heels along the trail.

Clem stopped abruptly. "Girlie, you stay up on the trail. I'm goin' down to the river 'n' take a wash." He pulled a big bar of yellow soap out of his pocket as he talked.

All the boys followed him to the river except Jim. Jo wrinkled up her nose. "I think he needs a bath. He should shampoo his whiskers too." Turning to Jim, she announced, "I'm going back to camp. You want to come?"

"OK."

They started back, but Jim changed his mind and decided to go with the boys. Jo shrugged her shoulders and continued on alone. She thought, *Mitsy is with Carlos. I'm glad she likes him. He doesn't have anyone but kid friends.*

It seemed strange, walking along the trail alone, almost like back on the farm when she had no one to play with. She used to imagine hordes of kids running through the trees, yelling, "Come on, Jo!" She smiled to herself. "I like camping out and having friends, even if we don't have the things we had on the farm.

Suddenly Jo heard yipping and barking. Turning, she saw Clem's dogs up the trail. Jack was in the lead. They didn't look like the obedient pets that had jumped out of Clem's truck. They looked ferocious! Jo's muscles froze, and her face felt stiff. Were they coming after *her?* Dogs did attack people. Her scalp tingled as she rolled under the fence and ran fast around the woodpile. Soon Jack and one of the other dogs snarled close behind her. She hit her foot against a chunk of wood. She *must* not fall—they would jump her. She couldn't run any faster; she couldn't yell for help—her throat was too dry.

It seemed like the dogs were practically on top of her when Carlos came running around the woodpile. Swerving to the left, he threw a slab of wood and hit Jack in the side. Yelping, the dog slunk away. Carlos kept throwing wood at the other dogs. They seemed glad enough to follow their leader to the pickup.

Out of breath and exhausted, Jo fell to the ground. She clutched the grass in her hands in an effort to calm herself. "They're gone. I'm safe. Thank you, Carlos," she said breathlessly.

Just then Clem crawled under the fence with his shirt in his hand and his beard dripping. He yelled all his bad words at Carlos, who still had a slab of wood in his hand. He yelled even when he came close. "Don't throw no more wood at them dogs. If she hadn't a-run, they wouldn't have chased her."

Carlos yelled back, "Those dogs acted mean! You said yourself: 'Trouble, there they go to gang up on somebody.' They were going to tear into Jo!"

Clem fumed. "That's a lie! Can't even take a wash in peace. I'll wipe the ground with you!" He stepped menacingly toward Carlos, still cussing.

Jo pulled up the grass she had in her hand. Surely the man knew the dogs wanted to attack her. Carlos shook the slab of wood in his hand at Clem. "You leave me alone! Don't come any closer."

John and his brothers came running around the woodpile with Mitsy right behind them. John panted, "Why don't you quiet down? There's going to be bad trouble if you don't. The camp boss'll be down our necks."

Mitsy came to Jo. She licked her hands and whined. Jo put her arms around her. "It's all right now." Suddenly she remembered her shirt and checked the sleeves for tears. They were OK. She better be more careful. The kids would think she was a leper if they ever saw her arms.

Clem put his dogs into the truck and started the

engine. Before driving down the camp road, he yelled out the window, "I'll get you for cruelty to animals and for runnin' away from your old man. I happen to know Shorty."

Carlos's face froze as he watched the truck disappear. He sat down by Jo. "I made a mistake. I blabbed about myself. He seemed to like me. He even asked me to travel with him. All the time, he planned on turnin' me over to Shorty. Of course, he may not even know Shorty."

John said, "Probably not."

Jerry added, "He's just blowin'."

Jo worried, "Will Shorty be back?"

Chapter Nine

And then Grandma came.

Uncle Matt drove her car. She had a nice car with roll windows, and Jo liked to ride in it, but Uncle Matt decided to pick pears with Mom and Daddy. Grandma couldn't drive.

Jo had fun with Grandma, though. Grandma made a checkerboard on top of a box and used buttons for the "men," as she called them. She made you work and think to win. You had to be alert to play checkers with her.

Jo often said, "I wish Dort would come back from wherever she went."

Grandma said, "You and Dort would play with the boys if she was here. You might as well play with them now. They seem like nice kids, and the little Mexican boy is very mannerly."

One day Grandma said, "We'll walk to that little berg and get some library books. I like to read."

It was three miles, and the sun seemed to get hotter every step of the way. Jo thought they would never get there. The library was upstairs in the department store. It had a desk for the librarian who, Grandma said, watched them like a hawk. The shelves were long and labeled: the bottom one for preschool children, the next one for primary and juniors. The other shelves had books for adults.

Jo felt shocked when Grandma argued with the librarian, who pulled her glasses off and stared at Grandma with her mouth partly open. She finally said, "We can't check books out to people without a permanent address. It's the rule."

Grandma said, "I don't plan on skipping the country with your books. I merely want to read and return them."

The librarian looked at her for a long time. Then she said, "You seem honest. You may go ahead and check out what you want."

"Thank you," Grandma said. She chose two books.

As they were going down the library steps Grandma muttered, "An act of Congress to get a few books!"

Grandma took Jo to a place she called an ice-cream parlor. They chose one of the little round tables by the window and sat down. Grandma had a dish of vanilla ice cream, and Jo had strawberry.

As they walked back to the camp they passed near a deep irrigation ditch with a scraggly tree by it. Grandma said, "Let's sit on those big rocks under the tree and rest a while."

They sat down, and Grandma fanned herself with an envelope she took out of her purse. Jo glanced down at her knee and screamed. "It's gone! He said it would go away. My wart's gone, Grandma! It's really gone!"

"What in the world are you so excited about?" Grandma asked.

Jo explained, "I had this ugly wart on my knee. The dishrag didn't make it go away."

Grandma laughed. "What did?"

"An old man rubbed sand on it and talked to the moon.

He said when I forgot about the wart, and then remembered it, it would be gone. He told the truth. It's gone!"

Grandma looked angry. "Jo, didn't your mother ever tell you not to monkey with hocus pocus like that? It's dangerous."

"No, Grandma."

"Stay away from that man."

"I have to. They moved out the next day."

"Good."

The boys came over as soon as they walked into camp. Jo told them what Grandma said about the wart disappearing.

"She's right," John said. "The Bible lady said that kind of stuff was from the devil. He can do miracles, and some folks think it's done by God. If anyone takes credit for a miracle, you know it's a lie."

That evening Grandma explained that she and Uncle Matt had to leave the next morning as they were going to visit Mom and Uncle Matt's brother in Idaho.

Jo thought to herself, *Grandma has been in camp all day with me. She's seen things Mom and Daddy haven't. One day she said she knew 2 + 2 = 4 before she ever went to school . . . right after Carlos came around the tent from his hideaway. So she probably knows where he camps. Hope she doesn't tell Mom.*

Early the next morning Daddy said, "We must go to work. Sorry, folks; we can't afford to miss two days. Besides, they might hire someone else to take our places."

Grandma and Uncle Matt were soon packed and ready to go.

Grandma said, "Jo, you'll have to be responsible for

taking those library books back." She gave Jo a big hug. "That librarian would have a caniption fit if they didn't get returned."

Jo laughed. "I'll see to it. I'll get the boys to go with me."

"You do that, honey. And Jo, I'm sure everything will work out right for Carlos. He's a good boy."

Jo gave Grandma another squeeze and kissed her goodbye. Grandma knew about Carlos, but she had kept quiet and didn't tell Mom and Daddy.

Outside the tent Uncle Matt grabbed Jo and swung her around and around. "You be good, kid."

They all laughed and waved, but Jo felt like crying. It seemed lonely now. She decided to ask the boys to go with her to return the library books. The boys agreed to go, but of course Jerry grumbled. "That's a long way to walk and it's getting hot already."

Jo said, "We can wear our bathing suits and go swimming on the way back."

They arrived at the department store, hot and tired. Mitsy followed them through the door as they headed for the stairs leading to the library. A fussy-looking man, who smelled like lemon, hurried to them. "Take the dog out! No scroungy dogs allowed in the store. What do you kids want?"

Carlos handed the books to Jo and picked up Mitsy. "I'll wait outside."

Jim and Jerry followed him.

John looked the man straight in the eyes. "This is a store. Are you refusing us as customers?"

"Don't be impudent."

"Is it impudent to ask a question? If it is, you were impudent and rude the way you asked us what we wanted."

The man stood with his mouth open as John turned to Jo. "I'll wait with the others."

Jo stiffened her back, said not a word, and sailed up the stairs to the library. At the desk she removed the books from the sack and placed them before the librarian. "My grandmother asked me to return these."

The librarian said, "Oh, she may keep them two weeks."

"Grandma went on a trip and said I should return them right away."

The lady smiled. Jo smiled back, then turned and went down the stairs.

The clerk met her at the bottom step. "Why didn't you say why you were in the store?"

Jo bit her lip and tried to remember all the things Daddy said to do when you're angry.

The man waited, and she continued thinking.

He said, "Well?"

Jo twisted her hair and said, "I didn't feel like it." She went outside to join the others.

Jim said, "I'm hot and tired. Can we go swimming?"

"As fast as we get to the river," John answered.

They were very quiet, each one thinking their own thoughts as they walked. At last Jo asked, "John, where did you get the nerve to speak up to the man in the store?"

"Dad never lets anyone put him down. He says we boys are never to get the idea that we aren't as good as anyone else. He says that we're clean, honest, and good citizens."

They were concentrating so much on what John said

that Shorty's old Chevy was practically on top of them before they saw it.

Jerry saw it first and said, low in his throat, "Jiggers, Carlos! It's Shorty."

Shorty stopped across the road from them and yelled, "Where's the Mex kid that hangs out with you kids?"

No one answered. No one looked around to see if Carlos was there.

"Cagey, ain't you? Tell him he better show."

Just then Mitsy yipped from some tall weeds. Jerry bounded toward the weeds and grabbed Mitsy. He brought her to Jo. He said, "She better stay in the road or a snake might bite her."

Shorty snorted and rattled on past them.

John called, "Come on out Carlos. He's gone."

Carlos ran out of the tall weeds and started picking thorns from his clothes. John slapped him on the shoulder. "When did you see him? Nobody else knew he was around."

"I didn't see him. I heard him. I know the sound of that car's rattles."

They continued walking until they came to the turn off to the swimming place at the river. Then they started running, as if they hadn't just walked six miles. Soon they had their clothes jerked off and were splashing in the water. They all swam out to the deep water, with Mitsy following.

Suddenly Carlos ducked and swam under water. Jo glanced to the shore and saw Shorty walking around, talking to people. Carlos stuck his head up for air. Mitsy paddled to shore, and Jo followed. The boys saw Shorty and swam close to Carlos. They all climbed out of the water and mingled with some Indian kids. Shorty couldn't recognize any of them at that distance. He soon got in his car and rattled away.

Carlos mused, "He's gone to get booze. He gets a bottle if anything stops him from having his own way. He wants me for some reason. I wonder what."

That night Mom asked Jo if she had taken Grandma's books back. Jo answered, "Of course."

Jo hadn't minded the walk. In fact, she had forgotten about it, but not about Shorty. Why did he keep showing up, bothering them? It seemed to her that a man should be able to earn money without a boy's help. Maybe Shorty wanted Carlos for something else.

And why didn't Dort's family come back? Had something happened to them? She had many things to talk over with God that night.

Chapter Ten

All day Thursday Jo puzzled about where Dort and her family could be. Finally, in the evening, the girls and their father drove in and stopped by Jo's camp.

They jumped out of the car, and the father said, "I took my wife to the hospital early Sunday morning. The baby's OK, but Mother's awful sick. I'm mighty worried."

Jo's mom said, "Oh, dear! Where is she?"

"I took her to the county hospital. They didn't want her, because we're transients, but they finally cut all the red tape and let her in."

Daddy asked, "Will they take proper care of her?"

"The doc said she needed a specialist to operate. No money for that, of course. I'm about whipped."

Jo glanced from Dort's father to the girls. It seemed fruit tramps had all kinds of problems. Money was the biggest trouble—money for babies, doctor bills, groceries, and everything.

Mom inquired, "Did the baby come early?"

"Yes; a month, I believe. Probably climbing ladders did it. We knew better, but—"

Daddy interrupted, "Are you going back this evening?"

"Yes. I wondered if you folks would kinda keep an

eye on Dort and Tiny for the next couple days. I'll go to work from the hospital. The girls got tired of being cooped up in the car."

Jo smiled at Dort when Mom said "Yes."

John's father called from their truck steps, "How much do you need for the operation?"

"If I had $100 they'd go ahead and operate. Where'll I get that much? We got our money from last week. I bought groceries, gas, and parts to fix the car. You know how it is—broke again." He paused. "Well, I'll be back in a couple days. Just send the girls to bed. They'll be OK."

Jo put her arms around Tiny and Dort. "I didn't know your mama was going to have a baby."

Dort smiled. "Mama said to keep still about it. It's a boy. Daddy's glad. He said we need another man in the family."

Jo glanced over at John's camp. His mother was taking face powder, hand cream, and other things out of a cigar box. She handed the box to John's father. He brought it over and said to Daddy, "Come on, Bruce. Let's see if there's a hundred bucks in this camp." He put four quarters and a dollar bill in the box. Daddy added three more dollar bills, and they started down the camp road.

"Is it for Dort's mother, to pay the doctor?" Jo asked.

"Yes," Mom answered.

"Daddy worked 10 whole hours for three dollars, didn't he?"

"Just about, but he's strong, and we must help."

Jo ran into the tent. She pulled her box of special things from under her cot. She brought out a little tin box, opened it, and counted out some change. "Fifty cents," she said aloud.

Dort watched her from the door. "What are you going to do?"

"Put it in the box for your mom's operation. God's using us to help your mother."

The girls raced to catch up with the men. Jo put her money in the box. Daddy smiled. "That's my girl."

The girls went back to camp. They sat down on the grass with the boys to wait for the men. Everybody wanted them to come back with enough money for Dort's mother to have the operation.

John and Carlos wrestled. Jim and Jerry played a game with a pocketknife. Tiny talked about the new baby. Dort sat quietly. Jo craned her neck this way and that, watching for the men. Finally they came back. The kids jumped up asking, "How much? How much?"

Daddy said, "A lot of people finished their jobs and don't know what they'll be doing next. They're afraid to let go of a nickel. Some aren't in camp."

All the time Daddy talked, Slim, John's father, counted the money. "Thirty-eight dollars and 40 cents. Not bad for about 85 camps. I'll ask at work tomorrow. You do the same, Bruce. Be sure and ask the boss."

"Will do," Daddy agreed.

The next morning Dort and Tiny joined Carlos and Jo for breakfast. Mom left scrambled eggs, fried potatoes, and a bag of pears. Mom and Dad were picking pears now, so they brought some home every night.

John and his brothers came over as they were finishing

their dishes. They cleared the table off and started to play a game. Dort looked sad. She said, "I don't think they'll get enough money. What if my mama dies? She might."

Carlos looked thoughtful. "Did you ever hear of a benefit program?"

Jo answered, "At home they had a benefit party for a man who got crippled in the woods. They sold tickets and gave the money to his family."

Jerry exclaimed, "We could have a party on the platform and give the money to Dort's folks."

John said, "People in camp wouldn't buy tickets; things happening on the platform are always free."

Carlos looked wise. "Yes, but we could get 'em there and take up a collection."

Jo grew excited. "Let's start up a talent show. There hasn't been one for a long time. Mitsy can do the tricks—I've been teaching her."

John laughed. "We'll dress Carlos up funny. He can announce the numbers on the program."

"Why me?" Carlos asked, grinning.

"Oh, you'd be good!" John laughed.

Jo looked around at the eager faces. They all wanted to help. "We can go around and tell everybody in camp. The bigger the audience, the more we'll collect." She planned out loud.

John said, "I'll get Dad to explain what the money's for."

Dort smiled. "All this for my mother! You're good friends."

John said grimly, "We gotta stick together or the big machine'll get us."

Jo asked, "What machine?"

John frowned. "You can tell you haven't been a fruit tramp very long. There's a big machine out there. It grinds away, making us hungry, sick, broke, and keeps us from having homes."

"Oh," Jo said. "It took our farm. I guess you mean the Depression."

"Yeah," John muttered.

Carlos said, "Aw, let's get down to business. Remember the last boxing matches? They put a sign up at the station saying boxers from anywhere could participate. That brought in outsiders. Let's make a sign. We'll rip up a cardboard box and write on it."

Dort said, "We can't have it tonight. That wouldn't be time enough for everybody to see the sign."

John said, "Right. Let's get the sign up now and have it in two nights. That's two days' advertising. Saturday night's a good time for it. Come on, Carlos, we'll get a box at the gas station."

"I have color crayons to make the sign," Jo offered.

While the boys were gone, she rummaged in her box for the colors, then sat down with Jim, Jerry, and the girls.

Dort looked at Tiny. "Would you do your stunts?"

"Not in front of people!" Tiny protested.

Jo wondered what Tiny's stunts could be. "Show me, Tiny. No one is here but us."

Tiny answered, "For you, Jo." She tucked the bottom of her dress into the top of her panties and started turning cartwheels up and down between John and Jo's camps. Then she did handsprings and spun around on her toes. She did forward rolls, log rolls, and more cartwheels. She ended by doing the splits.

Jo clapped her hands. "Where did you learn all that?"

Dort answered for Tiny. "We lived in an old store, close to another building, last school year. Downstairs in the building a lady taught acrobatics and dances. We watched through the window. At home Tiny practiced what the lady taught. She did better than anyone in the class."

Jo said, "If the show's good, people will put more money in the box for your mama's operation. Then she can come back sooner. Do your stunts at the talent show, Tiny, please."

Jim said, "If I knew how, I'd do it for my mother if she needed me."

Tiny frowned.

Jo thought, *No wonder they call her Tiny. Right now she looks 3, not 5.*

Tiny's frown grew deeper; then it disappeared, and she smiled. "I'll do it for Mama."

Dort and Jo grabbed Tiny and kissed her. Dort said, "You're a good little sister."

The boys brought the box, cut it open, and trimmed it with Carlos' knife.

Jo said, "I'm good at printing. Let me do it!" With much help and many suggestions, she wrote in huge letters at the top: TALENT SHOW. Then in smaller letters: Anybody from camp or outside, bring your talent and do it!" The time came next: Saturday Night at 7:30, August __.

Jerry had to run to the station to find out the date. Jo added "20" in the space after August. One more sentence was needed: Name your talent and sign here. She left plenty of room for people to sign.

They ran up to the station with the sign. The old man

said, "H'mmmm," and nailed it on the outside wall for them.

John said, "We'll make a big thing of it. Talk to everybody, and let's put a sign up at the river where we swim. Lots of folks from all over go swimming there."

They made another sign. At the bottom it said: Sign up at the camp service station.

John said, "Jerry, get a couple nails out of Dad's box."

Jo suggested, "We can put our swimming suits on. Might as well swim. We can dress when we get back."

Everyone agreed, changed into their suits, and started out. Jo had her shirt over her suit, as usual. At the river they located a cottonwood tree all the swimmers would pass on their way to the water. Carlos held the sign on the trunk of the tree, Jerry held the nails, and John pounded them in with a rock.

Just as they finished the job, Jo recognized the boy who had pushed Mitsy under the water. He came toward them, so she held Mitsy close to her side.

The boy said, "Who do you think you are, hanging that sign up? Anybody'd think you were running that show. Does the camp boss know what you're up to?"

Jo watched Carlos turn around. Would he remember what she told him about getting even and about staying out of trouble?

Carlos eyed the boy up and down. "Yes, he knows. Why don't you sign up for your act? Call it 'Big Nose.' Show how you stick your nose into everybody's business."

Jo peered at the boy. Now what would he do?

He retorted, "Ha! I'm going to tell your dad where you hang out. He's going to give me a dollar if I do. How's that, Mex?"

"In that case, mongrel, I might as well lick you, be-ings you ask for it every time I see you. Can you take it?"

Jo held her breath. The boy was bigger than Carlos; Carlos should have paid attention to her. She told him to stay out of trouble and all that stuff about vengeance.

Suddenly Carlos extended his fists and began danc-ing around the boy in quick steps. The boy seemed to be more in the mood for rough and tumble. He crouched close in on Carlos, but couldn't seem to find an opening.

Carlos yelled, "Now see what happens to a nose that's where it doesn't belong!" Then with his right fist he flashed a cutting blow to the other boy's nose.

Jo stepped farther back as Carlos continued to dance around. Quicker than before, he jabbed the boy on the nose again.

Jo glanced around. A crowd had gathered. They yelled and called out to the one they wanted to win.

She noticed how Carlos quickly changed his foot-work. Instead of dancing around the boy, he jumped to-ward him. The boy kept hitting at Carlos. All at once Carlos beat down the other boy's waving fists and punched him with his left fist. Then both boys stumbled on stones and fell down. As they rolled around on the ground a man came up and pulled them apart. He stood between them as they stood up. "Now you baby roosters cool off and make up. And I don't care who started it."

Jo wondered if they would fight again the next time they met.

The man shook them. "Hurry up!"

Carlos grinned. "Sure; but he can remember this— my name is Carlos. He can keep out of my business too."

The boy smeared blood on his face as he swiped it with his hand. "OK. My name's Norman, and I never told anything to your pop. I didn't want his dollar."

(Jo saw that everyone was reading the sign. "Good!" she exclaimed to no one in particular. She shifted her attention back to the boys.)

"Is that true?" Carlos was asking.

"Sure, I just said that. Besides, I'm sorry I shoved the dog under the water. I didn't want to hurt her. I like to tease."

Carlos laughed. "Well, come on, Norm. Go swimming with us."

Norman kicked off his jeans, gave his swimming trunks a hitch, and followed the boys into the water. Jo sat on shore and held Mitsy. Dort and Tiny stayed with her.

Norman called out, "Honest; I won't hurt your dog. I wish my dog were here. A guy ran over him on purpose. He said 'It's just a fruit tramp's dog.'"

Jo said, "I'm sorry." She called Mitsy into the water with her. All that getting even, when all Norman needed was a friend. How mean of someone to say, "It's just a fruit tramp's dog."

Jo sighed. The thing to do was make enough money at the talent show. Would they?

Chapter Eleven

Excitement filled the whole camp the night of the program. Jo could barely sit through the evening meal. She talked and talked about the talent show until Daddy told her to calm down.

John's father came over. Daddy said, "I hope the kids make it tonight. I only collected $5 today. How much did you get?"

"I got $6 all together. Let's see . . . $38 plus $6 is $44, plus $5 more makes $49.40. Looks like they ought to get $50 dollars from the show, that is, if towners show up."

Jo made ruffles out of paper bags and colored them. She put one around Mitsy's neck and little ones above her feet. She pinned one around her own neck and put a bow in her hair. (She would be giving Mitsy directions.)

Dort said, "You look like a show person. All you need is a pretty blouse to go with the ruffles."

Quickly, Jo answered, "My shirt's fine. Bright blue will show up." She thought pretty blouses always seemed to have short sleeves.

Jo and Dort decided Tiny should wear her bathing suit. Jo said, "I'm glad it's red. It will show up good."

John loaned Carlos a pair of bib overalls and a big shirt. The girls stuffed pillows inside the pants to make him look fat. Jo smeared white poison ivy ointment all over his face and made big red lips with lipstick. She pulled an old straw hat over his head. "There! Now you *really* look funny. You'll make a good announcer."

Jerry said, "You'll have to ham it up, Carlos, like the other guys do at shows."

"I know," Carlos replied.

John and Jo looked over the list of those who had signed up for the program. Jo exclaimed, "Fifteen acts! It's going to be a good show." She grabbed Dort's hand, and they whirled around, laughing.

John said, "Here, Carlos, take your list."

Carlos glanced at the list. The fourth number startled him. It said: "Norman and brother, Tracy—a musical." He wondered what it was going to be. Norman and Tracy were good guys, but what would they do?

Before they left for the platform, Daddy asked, "Can you kids sing?"

They looked at him in surprise. Jo asked, "Why?"

"You better have something going while Slim and I collect the money."

Mom said, "I'll stand with the kids, and we'll ask the audience to sing old favorites with us."

The kids agreed, as long as Jo's mom would be with them.

Seven-thirty! Carlos wobbled out to the middle of the platform. His pillows bumped up and down. Jo hoped his face wouldn't melt off. "Glad all you fine people could make it to this great show!" he announced. "First on the program tonight is the internationally-known trick dog, Mitsy, and her owner, Jo."

Jo held Mitsy tight and tried to remember everything she had read in the book about how to make a dog act reasonably. She looked around from the edge of the platform. It seemed as though hundreds of people stared back at her. Why had she decided to do this?

Carlos yelled, "Come on, Jo!"

She *had* to do it. She carried Mitsy to the center of the platform. She laid down the big round hoop that John had made from a willow branch and sat Mitsy in front of her. Mitsy looked around at the crowd of people, then jerked away and started running around the edge of the platform, barking. Jo ran after her, but Mitsy zigzagged to Carlos.

Amid all of the laughing, Jo got Mitsy to sit up for a dog treat. She jumped back and forth through the hoop several times, but looked away when Jo said, "Roll over." Then she folded her paws and bowed her head.

Everyone clapped as Jo slipped the leash on Mitsy and led her away. She stood nearby to watch the other performers. Once her glance shifted from a group singing Western songs to the audience, straight across the platform. Her heart thudded. There stood Shorty with his eyes right on Carlos. He knew who the announcer was.

Jo thought, *He's mean. What shall I do? I can't yell, "Hey, Carlos, get wise. Shorty's here!"*

John came through the crowd to her side. "Do you see who I see?"

John always seemed to be right there when anybody needed help. She wondered if he ever got frightened or felt like screaming. She supposed not. She said, "Yes, I see him. He knows it's Carlos. The pillows and white face don't fool him."

Jo held Mitsy in her arms, but the dog wanted down. She wiggled and squirmed and gave a little bark every now and then.

John said, "Mitsy wants to be with Carlos. You can tell by the way she acts. Look, Jo, we have to warn Carlos. All of us must watch and stand around him when it's over. Shorty might catch him if we don't help."

Mitsy squirmed again.

"Let her down. You can chase her. She'll go to Carlos," John suggested.

Jo said, "I get it. Be sure and watch. She might run off."

"No, she wants to see why Carlos has been up there so long."

The Western singers left the platform. During the clapping, Jo let Mitsy down. Yipping and barking, she raced to Carlos and sniffed at him.

Jo ran after her. Carlos grabbed the leash and handed it to Jo when she reached the stage. She whispered, "Shorty's here. We'll stick close."

Carlos muttered, "Thanks." He said in a loud voice, "A famous dog like Mitsy wants to be in the act all the time."

The program continued. Carlos announced people as someone famous from New York, San Francisco, or Los Angeles. He said one singing group ended their job by traveling through Europe.

"The next thing on the program," Carlos called, "is a surprise to all of us. I didn't think they would make it, but here they are—Norm and Tracy, straight from New York. Get ready for a special musical by the brothers."

Norman walked out on the platform with a small button accordian. Tracy followed with another one like it. Norman said, "Our instruments are small. See if you can keep up with us." They started playing, nothing "ho-downy," just sweet, musical sounds that kept your feet moving.

Everyone clapped, so they played a second number. Then they bowed and left the platform. Jo clapped longer than anyone; Norman and his brother could really play! The second number had sounded like a creek and clouds and birds. Anyway, it made her think of that.

Jo thought, *Surely, we'll get enough money. Everything's going fine . . . if only old Shorty would leave.*

Tiny's act came last. She walked out to the middle of the platform, spun around on her toes, and looked at everybody. Jo felt sorry for her. She looked frightened. She hoped Tiny would go ahead with her act. She blurted out in a high, squeaky voice, "I'm doing this for my mama, 'cause she's terribly sick." Then she did cartwheels all around the platform, log rolled across forward, then rolled back. She did handsprings from one end of the platform to the other. After each stunt she spun around on her toes.

Jo breathed deeply. Tiny did a fine act. She looked cute in her bathing suit. During the clapping, Jo and her friends—even Norman and Tracy—got on the platform with Mom.

Quietly, John told them that Shorty was there. He said, "After it's over, stay circled around Carlos all the time."

John's father said in a big booming voice, "Ladies and gentlemen, the little girl who said she was performing for her mama told the truth. Her family lives here in camp. Her mother was taken to the hospital Sunday. Tiny has a new baby brother, but she won't have a mother unless she has an operation. Bruce and I took up a collection in camp and where we work. We got $49.40. We need at least $50 more. Besides, you know how expenses pile up when someone's sick. We thought you might like to help out. Bruce and I are coming around with our hats while you sing."

Jo heard Mom say, "Tiny, do your cartwheels around the platform during the songs."

Tiny nodded her head and went around the platform twice.

Mom got everybody singing "America," "Aunt Rhody's Old Gray Goose," "Seeing Nellie Home," "Red River Valley," and others. She asked those in the crowd for suggestions. They ended up with, "What'll We Do When the Pond Goes Dry."

The men came to the platform, jingling the money in their hats. Daddy called out, "'Big Rock Candy Mountains,' folks. Sing it loud and clear!"

After the song John's father yelled, "Thank you, everyone. It's been a great night."

All Jo's friends stayed close beside Carlos on the way to camp. Carlos took his costume off and washed his face. Jo pulled the ruffles off Mitsy and herself.

Daddy said, "Well, kids, you got $76.21. With the $49.40, that makes $125.61 cents!" He smiled at Dort and Tiny. "Your mom's going to be all right, girls."

Tears came to Dort's eyes, and she squeezed Tiny until the little girl said, "Ouch!"

Jo said, "God used all of us to help."

Carlos whispered to John, "I wonder where Shorty went."

John said, "Maybe he left."

"Not him," Carlos murmured, and slipped away to his hiding place.

Jo wished Carlos could stay with her family and not be bothered with Shorty. "I'll ask God to take care of Carlos," she whispered.

Chapter Twelve

Slim, John's father, herded his family to bed. Jo noticed that John forgot to get his big overalls that Carlos had borrowed. She picked them up for him, but he had already disappeared into their little house.

Dort pulled on her arm. "Jo, it's lonesome with just Tiny and me. Do you suppose your mom would let you sleep at my camp? We could all three get into Mom and Dad's big bed."

Jo was surprised when Mom said, "I think that's a good idea. Sleep late, girls. You've had a big night. I'll leave breakfast for you."

Jo kissed Mom good night, grabbed Dort's arm, and they crossed the road, giggling. Dort turned on a flashlight, and they started getting ready for bed in the dim light. Tiny undressed and put on a thin, worn night gown. Dort jerked her clothes off and pulled an old dress over her head.

She said, "I have another old dress; it's clean. You can sleep in it."

Jo stood in the middle of the tent, horrified. None of Dort's dresses had sleeves! She couldn't take her shirt off, but Mom would have a fit if she slept in it. An idea came to her. "Hey, Dort, look! I've still got John's overalls."

Dort laughed. "I hope you don't prefer sleeping in them to my dress."

Jo giggled and said, "No." She slipped the overalls on. "Stuff me with pillows," she commanded. "I want to look like Carlos did."

They felt around in the feeble light until they found pillows to put inside the front and back of the pants.

Dort warned, "Be careful and don't pull the thread on the end of the pillow in front. It's about to come apart. Mama was going to sew it, but she didn't get to it."

Jo said, "I'm going after my pajamas. Mom and Daddy will think the program is still going on!"

Tiny cried out, "My tummy hurts. My back hurts. Dort, rub my back, please?"

Tiny lay down on the big bed and Dort started rubbing her back. She turned to Jo. "You better not go after your pajamas. If it was my mother, she'd say, 'Beings you're running back and forth, you can stay home.'"

Jo replied, "Oh, Mom won't say that. Come with me."

Tiny quavered, "Don't go!"

"I'll go alone," Jo said. "Be back in a jiff."

Dort said, "You won't be back. Your mom will make you stay."

Jo laughed and ran across the road and into her tent. The pillows bumped all the way. Mom and Dad were not impressed with her outfit. Daddy said, "Jo, we must work tomorrow. Get your stuff and scoot to bed, or else stay here." Then he turned the gas lantern out and crawled into bed with Mom, who was almost asleep.

Jo grabbed the straw hat Carlos had worn and put it on. She thought, *I better go in a hurry. I can put my paja-*

*mas on without Dort seeing my arms, because she'll proba-
bly turn off the flashlight.*

She grabbed her pajamas and ran halfway across the
road just as a car came out of nowhere. She turned back
to wait until it had passed. The car stopped. The door
opened. A man stepped out and clapped his hand over
her mouth. He pulled her into the car, raking the pillows
on the door. Jo couldn't scream. Any noise she made
sounded like gargling. The man kept his hand over her
mouth as he drove past the gas station. He said, "Now
shut up, or I'm going to slap you one you won't forget.
Remember, I can do it!"

Jo had never been spoken to that way. She shuddered as she glanced at him. *Shorty!* In a flash she knew
what had happened. With the pillows and the overalls,
he had thought she was Carlos.

Calming down, she thought, *If I can get his hand
away, I'll tell him he's made a mistake.* She pushed, pried,
and squirmed—and finally bit his hand. He flung her
into the corner with such force she hit the door handle.

"Don't ever try anything like that again," Shorty snarled.

Jo wondered if her head was cut. Oh, where were
they going? Mom and Dad would worry— No, they
wouldn't! They thought she was at Dort's, Dort would
tell them— No, she probably thought Mom had made
her stay home! Oh, why had she dressed up like Carlos?
Why did she worry about her arms? It wasn't as if she
could help what they looked like. Tears ran down her
face. She started whimpering and catching her breath.

Shorty kept his eyes on the road. He said, "I didn't
know you were a bawl baby. Shut up and keep still. See

that letter stickin' out of the book on the seat? That's from a bank in Sacramento. Your folks put money away for you. With the interest, there's $300 now. I took care of you and your mother, and I want that money. We'll get it, see. And you're not to let out a peep or I'll knock you cold."

Jo tried to stop crying. If he'd only look at her. . . . But he wouldn't. She started to ask him to, but he interrupted. "Nary a word, Mexican. As soon as we get to Sacramento, I'll get that money, let you go, and hope I never see you again."

The car lights seemed dim. All she could see was a long stretch of road and what appeared to be sagebrush. They turned off the highway onto a small gravel road and went downhill and around curves until they stopped by the river. Her heart sank as she saw the sign, "Maryhill Ferry." She shuddered. He'd take her across the river. How would she ever get back? She had heard somewhere that when kidnappers got frightened, they killed their victims. When Shorty found out his mistake, what would he do?

Jo felt her head. It hurt. Everything seemed fuzzy, and she had a scary feeling in her chest. Her head nodded back and forth, her eyes closed, then opened with a jerk. She finally closed them again and sank against the seat, thinking, *Yes, he's a mean man.*

Chapter Thirteen

Jo opened her eyes, puzzled. She felt of her head. Ouch! That bump hurt. Then she remembered what had happened: Shorty had pulled her into his car. He had slammed her against the door post when she tried to fight him. Had she gone to sleep, or what?

She realized they were parked when she heard Shorty start the engine. She glanced outside quickly. They had crossed the river and were leaving the ferry. She started to tell Shorty about his mistake, then closed her mouth so fast her teeth jarred each other. What would Shorty do when he found out? Would he harm her? Would he let her go? Would he take her back? She frowned. John always said, "Fruit tramps use their wits, because they don't have any money. Besides, nobody trusts them."

How can I get out of this car? Jo wondered. *If I get out, will Shorty chase me? If I were really Carlos, what would I do? Carlos uses his wits.*

A story she had read flashed into her mind. In the story, the kids had thrown red pepper in someone's face, causing the person to cough and sputter, giving the kids a chance to escape. She shrugged. She didn't have any red pepper.

She thought of another story about a kid who threw

sand in another kid's eyes. *I don't have anything to throw,* she thought. She squirmed around in the seat, shifting her body to the other side. She felt uncomfortable with the big pillows in her overalls.

Red pepper . . . Sand . . . She didn't have either. Suddenly she had an idea. *I can do it!* she thought.

She reached inside the bib of her overalls, and working very carefully, moved the front pillow until she had it where she could pull the threads on the seam. *A good thing Dort's mother hasn't gotten around to resewing it,* she thought. The material felt old and soft. She found the loose thread and, in the process, the old straw hat rubbed against the back of the seat and fell forward to the floor.

Shorty turned toward her, squinting. Then his eyes bugged out and bad words spewed from his mouth. He yanked the wheel to the right, pulled the car over, and slammed on the brakes. He sputtered, "Who are you?"

Use your wits! Use your wits! she kept telling herself. Out loud, she said, "I'm Jo. You wouldn't let me tell you before."

Shorty's voice boomed. "What am I going to do with you? I'm not a nursemaid."

Jo said, "You can take me back."

"No, I can't. You're trouble with a big T."

"You can let me go by myself."

"Sure, you'd fly right to this town ahead and tell the police. A *girl!* You've ruined everything."

Jo kept pulling on the thread in the pillow until she had the end open. Should she do it? She would try. She stalled. "Why did you leave Carlos in the first place, if you want him so bad?"

"Curious, ain't you? That's a girl."

Jo thought, *He doesn't remember telling me about the money.*

Shorty grumbled, "I sure don't need you."

To keep the conversation going, she asked, "Are you Carlos's father?"

Shorty spewed his breath out. "No, I ain't! What's that got to do with you?" He continued saying mean things about Carlos, his mother, and Jo.

While he talked, Jo carefully pulled the pillow from the overalls and opened it wide. She lifted it level with Shorty's head and gave the closed end a push to the inside. She gave it a second push, and a blizzard of feathers exploded in Shorty's face and flew all around him. She couldn't even see his head.

The man gasped and choked, sneezing as he pawed at the swirling feathers. Jo ducked his flailing arms, opened the door, and slipped out of the car. Shorty leaned over to grab her, but she dodged his hands and threw the empty pillow at him.

"I'll get you, you little smart alec!" he yelled after her. He opened the door on his side and started around the car.

Quickly, Jo climbed back into the car, the rear pillow slipping and sliding in her overalls. She grabbed the letter from the bank, slid under the wheel, and scooted out the door just as Shorty came around to the other side of the car. He hadn't seen her! She paused a second to catch her breath.

Shorty called, "You can't get far. I'm after you!" He ran down the road toward the ferry.

"He thinks I went that way," Jo whispered. She grabbed both sides of her rear pillow, so it wouldn't flop around, and ran toward the river. She ran until her teeth ached. Gasping, she sank down behind some bushes. Lying flat on her stomach, she peeked through the brush. She couldn't see anything. She put the envelope into her pocket. If she got back, Carlos could get his money.

She pulled the rear pillow out of her overalls, tucked it under her and waited. Had she used her wits, or would Shorty find her? As she lay there, her heartbeat slowed down and her breathing returned to normal. She waited and waited, trying to think what to do next. She didn't know how much time had gone by, but later she heard Shorty start his old car and drive toward the ferry. She decided, "I'd better stay here. He's still looking for me."

She glanced down. The buttons were gone from the cuff of her left sleeve, exposing a zigzagging brown spot, even in the dark. She rolled the sleeve up, then unbuttoned the other cuff and rolled that sleeve up too. She said out loud, "Those spots are me. They aren't important now. The important thing is to get back to camp."

Soon she heard the Chevy come back, slowly. It went back and forth several times. After a while Jo thought, *I think he's gone, but I'm not sure.* She shivered. "It's creepy. I wonder what time it is. I wonder when anyone will miss me. How will I get across the river? Shorty probably asked the ferryman if he saw me."

Jo's mind began to dwell on other things: the farm, the baby calf, Mama's geese, kitty cat, and the times grandma visited. Grandma said she knew how Jo felt about not having a brother. Grandma didn't have any brothers or sisters either. She told how happy she had been when her cousin came to live with them. She had someone to play with and go to school with then. Of course, they lived on a big farm, and Grandma's father didn't need a job.

Slowly she relaxed and fell asleep.

When she woke up, the sun was shining on her face. She squirmed around. Her body felt stiff from lying on the hard ground, and her head still hurt. Cautiously, she peered from her hiding place: nothing in sight. She stood up, stuck her hand deep into her pocket and felt the envelope. The whole thing was true. She hadn't been dreaming. If for no other reason than the letter, Shorty would try to find her.

She whispered, "God, the lady who visited around camp and gave away papers said many nice things about You. She said You'd take care of us if we asked. Please take care of me, God. Amen."

Jo picked up her pillow and walked to the highway. She turned left onto the gravel road that led to the ferry. She walked near the edge of the road, through the sagebrush, always ready to run if she should see Shorty's old Chevy.

How *would* she get across the river? Shorty probably told the ferryman he was her father and that she was a runaway. That's what he'd said about Carlos. Jo stooped over and rolled up the legs of John's overalls. They were loose and too long without the pillows to draw them up. She rubbed her forehead. The sun seemed to pound down on her. She sighed. "I wish I had a drink of water."

She looked ahead at the ferry crossing and decided

to hide near it and figure out what to do. Watching the road ahead and looking back often, she continued until she came to the ferry ramp. She saw nothing to hide behind, so made herself flat between sagebrush plants and pulled a tumble weed in front of her. She peeked through her prickly wall at the ferry chugging its way from the other side.

She glanced down at her arms in surprise. Were the spots getting lighter? She remembered that Mom had taken her to a doctor when she was in second grade. He had said the spots were not birthmarks. He said that if she stayed out of the sun they might get lighter. Was that why Mom always agreed when she wanted long sleeves and never commented when she didn't want the spots showing? Quickly, she rolled her sleeves down again. "Just in case," she muttered.

Jo saw a green car drive up and wait. She tried to make up her mind whether she should ask for a ride. Then she decided that wouldn't be using her wits. Shorty might come while they waited. With a desolate feeling, she watched the ferry come, get the green car, and start back. While the ferry slowly oozed over to the other side, a new truck slid to a stop near her hiding place. It had a load of empty boxes on it that was covered with a canvas. The canvas was loose on the corner next to her and flopped around as the truck stopped.

Jo thought, *If I really used my wits, I'd crawl under that canvas and ride to the other side without anyone knowing it. Would I get caught? Shorty might drive up behind the truck.* She wiped her face with the back of her hand. *Daddy says you can't do anything unless you try.* She waited a little longer, then peered out again. The ferry would soon be across. She glanced into the cab of the truck. The driver never looked up; he seemed to be reading a paper. She looked for other cars. Nothing coming. She slipped from her hiding place to the back of the truck and waited a second to see if the man had heard. He kept on reading his paper.

Carefully, she pushed her pillow under the canvas and hoisted herself onto the edge of the truck bed. She gave her overalls a hitch and slipped under the loose end of the canvas. She wished she could let her legs dangle over the end of the truck—there wasn't much room—but they would show. She tucked the canvas ends under her and waited for what seemed like hours, hardly breathing. She wiped rivulets of sweat from her face and whispered, "Better to swelter than to sit behind a tumble weed for the rest of my life."

Finally she heard a car leave the ferry. She felt the truck move as the man drove up on the ramp. The ferryman waited a while, then started across the river. Jo thought, *I must not move, no matter how many needles stick into me. I must not peek out, no matter how curious I am. I must get to camp.*

Then they were across. The truck climbed up the hill toward the highway. She started slipping as they went up. She grew frightened. She said out loud, "He's going too fast. I can't stay put. Will he stop? Oh, no! I'm going to fall off." She grabbed one of the ropes that held the boxes and bumped along. She bounced close to the edge. Maybe it would be better to give herself away. "Oh! Oh! Oh!"

She called out, "Stop! I'm back here!"

The truck didn't stop. The man couldn't hear her.

Chapter Fourteen

The morning after the talent show, Carlos woke up late. He frowned. "It's not always going to be good weather. Winter's coming. It snows here. Maybe I can pick hops, if they let kids pick without their folks. I have to make enough to go south."

Shrugging, he got up and thought about something else on his way to Jo's camp. "Good thing Jo's parents got a job that went right into apricots, peaches, and then pears. They're lucky. John's folks, too, and that makes it lucky for me."

John and Jerry were washing dishes. John called, "Hey, Carlos! Jo stayed at Dort's last night. They're not up yet. Come have some oats."

Carlos hurried over to John's and sat down at the picnic table. He watched John scrape cooked oatmeal from the pot into a dish and cover it with brown sugar. John said, "Sorry; the milk's all gone."

Carlos grinned. "I can taste the sugar better without the milk."

The boys discussed the program and the money that had been raised for Dort's mother. Then John said, "I think the girls took a powder last night. They've never slept this late before. They're probably talking and giggling in bed. That's the way our cousins do."

Norman called from the road. "Hi, everybody!" Tracy stood beside him.

"Hi, you big shots from New York, you famous musicians!" Jerry laughed.

"Come on over," John invited.

"Norm, how'd you guys learn to play the squeeze boxes?" Jerry asked.

Norm laughed. "Every winter since we could walk, Dad's had us practice. You ought to hear *him* play. He wanted *us* to play in the talent show though.

"Sure was good," Carlos said. They all nodded their heads.

"Did you hear Shorty driving around camp after the show last night?" Norm asked.

"No, I guess I slept through that one," Jerry said.

"Me, too," John added.

"When he came by our camp, I thought I'd tag after him and see what he was up to. I think everyone in camp had gone to bed. I about caught up to him when Dad yelled, "Norm!" He can yell. Believe me, I stopped. Shorty was just poking along, but I had to go back."

"I suppose we'll have a showdown eventually. Sometimes I think I might as well plain tell him that I'm not going with him anywhere. But he'd force me to anyway. He's short, but built like a bull. He can bat me around," Carlos explained.

"Well, be careful," Norm said. "We're moving out in the morning. Dad has a job up Naches way."

"It's good he has a job," John said, and the rest added, "Yeah."

They looked up as Dort and Tiny came across the road. Dort said, "I knew Jo'd never come back last night when she went after her pajamas. Isn't she up yet?"

She pulled Jo's tent flap back and called, "Are you alive?" Then she grew quiet.

"What's the matter?" Carlos asked.

Dort said slowly, "She's not here. Her bed's like it was yesterday."

Carlos looked puzzled. He walked toward the road, muttering to himself. "If Dort thought Jo stayed home, and Jo's folks thought she stayed with Dort, then where is she? Something must have happened!"

He glanced at the edge of the road. What was that? He picked up two pink garments.

Dort yelled, "That's her pajamas! She went back after them."

John said in a firm, calm voice, "Everybody come here and sit down."

They sat on the grass between Jo and John's tents.

John spoke. "Dort, let's get this straight. When did you see Jo last?"

Dort explained how Jo put on John's overalls, stuffed them with pillows, and went after her pajamas. "She wanted to fool her folks and make them think she was Carlos. I told Jo her mom would make her stay if she went home, and I thought that was what happened."

Carlos jumped up. His brown face looked pale. "This is Shorty's trick. He thought she was *me*, and he got her. She had on that old straw hat, foolin' around with it, when I left. She probably put it on again. The pillows in the overalls and the hat did it. She got her pajamas and started back. He got her! He thought she was me!"

Everybody looked at Carlos with frightened eyes.

Finally John asked Carlos, "Why would Shorty want you? I mean, do you have any idea?"

Carlos wrinkled his brow. "Only thing I can think of is to pick hops for him. It's about hop time. I'm a fast picker, and he's not worth his salt."

"You think that's where he's headed?"

"Might be. Shorty's mean. I've got to find Jo."

"Ever drive, Carlos?"

"You mean a car?"

"Yes."

"I drove for Mother when she was sick, before she married Shorty. After they got married and Shorty started acting wild, we'd go away sometimes, and I'd drive. She sold her car."

John thought hard. "We'll find Jo. Here's what we can do. Dad always keeps the keys to the truck, but I can start it another way. I've seen Dad do it. I'd drive, but you know how my eyes are. I see wrong. I don't have the corrective glasses they told me to get at school. You can drive, because I might have a wreck."

"I'll do it," Carlos said.

They followed John to the truck. "It's not really a truck. It's just a cut down Ford," John explained. "Dad built the house on it for us kids to sleep in—too many of us for the tent."

Carlos watched John get a jumper wire from the tool-box. It was about 20 inches long, with clips at each end. He started to lift the hood. Carlos said, "Better wait until that woman goes back into her tent. It's time for her to tie the boys up. She tells the camp boss everything. In fact, there are still a few people in camp. Some work's over, but most of them won't be up and around yet. They sleep late when they're not workin', so nobody'll try to stop us."

John hesitated until the woman went inside, then he raised the hood up and almost climbed on top of the engine. He attached one clip on the positive terminal on the battery, and the other to the battery connection on the coil. Then he lowered the hood.

Carlos asked, "Dort, will you stay and watch for Jo, in case she comes back?"

"Of course," Dort answered. "I have Tiny anyway."

John said, "Jim, you stay with Dort. Jerry, you come. We might have a fight and need somebody to help."

Norm said, "I can't go, but I'll keep my eyes open."

"Me, too," added Tracy. "We have to help break camp."

John folded up some old blanket pieces and put them on the driver's seat. "Now you can see better," he said to Carlos.

Carlos climbed behind the wheel, and Jerry got in the middle. John crawled in on the other side and slammed the door.

Carlos said, "Dort, be sure and tell Jo's folks what happened if they show up before we do. Tell 'em we're snoopin' the hops."

"We better get back first," John muttered.

Carlos glanced at him. John was letting himself in for a lot of trouble with his dad. He frowned. The kids were getting into all kinds of messes on account of him. He'd better not wreck the truck.

Carlos felt around for the starter button and pushed on it. The engine turned over, started, coughed, stopped, started again, and finally settled down to a steady rumble. He pressed his worn tennis shoe over the clutch, shifted into reverse, and backed away from the camp, then headed toward the gas station. It was too early for the old folks to be sitting out front.

The grumbling neighbor came out of her tent at the sound of the motor and began haranguing Dort. "What's that boy doing? I'm telling his dad when he gets home."

Carlos figured his driving experience didn't amount to much. He should have told John that he'd driven only four times on a straight-away. As long as they didn't have to go through town, he'd be all right. He'd take things as they came along. He headed north on the blacktop.

They had to find Jo. No telling about Shorty. He'd knocked him and his mother around every time he got a chance. He might do almost anything. *Boy, I've brought trouble,* he thought.

John said, "Carlos, there's a short cut to the hop country. What do you think?"

Carlos never took his eyes from the road. "I've never been there. We always picked in Oregon. Shorty probably doesn't know about the short cut, so maybe we could get there in time to catch him."

Jerry said, "It's not far to the ferry. Maybe Shorty crossed the river and headed for California. Maybe he doesn't plan to pick hops."

Carlos bit his lip. Jerry might be right. What would happen if Shorty took Jo to California? He said, "Let's go to the ferry. We'll see what's around, and if we don't find a clue we'll go to the hop country."

John nodded.

Jerry grumbled, "Probably never find 'em anyway."

John said, "Don't start that."

Carlos heard them bickering, but it didn't register. If Shorty hurt Jo, he'd get him good. But why would Shorty go to California? Was this a wild goose chase? Maybe they should go to the hops . . . No, better go to the ferry first.

The old Ford bounced along, rattling a chain in the back. Carlos's ankles ached from stretching his feet to reach the clutch and brake. He wanted his feet to be right there ready, in case of an emergency. He gripped the wheel hard, his knuckles white. He kept his eyes glued on the road until his eyeballs felt like they'd pop out. He couldn't drive along matter-of-fact like a grown man because every time he met a car his heart began to thump wildly.

A big sedan whizzed past them. A boy about John and Carlos's age turned and stared. He said something, and a man in the backseat looked out the rear window.

Jerry exclaimed, "They noticed that we're kids!"

Carlos frowned.

"I guess they're going to keep going on down the road," John muttered.

They passed a crossroads and a gas station. Carlos sighed with relief that there was no stop sign. He took a firmer grip on the wheel and pressed harder on the gas pedal. It wouldn't hurt them to speed up a little. They'd never find Shorty at this rate.

When they came to the turnoff to the ferry, Carlos made a left, careening the car around a couple curves, onto the gravel road. The car eased along for a way, then the engine died. Carlos looked at John; John looked at the gas gauge that didn't work.

Carlos felt frantic. He stomped on the gas pedal and pumped the hand choke like his mother used to do when her car balked. The engine started again, and they bumped along a few more yards, then it conked out again. Carlos's shoulders slumped. His arms shook not only from anxiety, but from how tightly he'd been gripping the wheel.

"We're out of gas," Jerry said. "We were about out when we came to this camp. That's why Dad and Mom started riding to work with someone else. Dad never used the truck, so he never got a fill-up. You dumbhead."

John said, "You should have mentioned it before we left camp. Now, be quiet."

"Sure, but we're a long way from camp. Dad'll come home before we get back with the truck—or without it."

John answered, "There's a long time before that, but if it happens that way I suppose you'll bawl-baby around."

Carlos suggested, "Maybe a wire slipped off."

They climbed out, and John lifted the hood. Carlos peered under, "Fits on perfect. Nothin's wrong. Just out of gas—and no money to buy any." He slammed the hood down.

Carlos kicked the gravel with his foot. "Shorty's probably found out his mistake by now. Jo's in for it, for sure. We have no money to get across the river on the ferry either. I should have thought things out before we started." He looked down the hill. Maybe he could get help from the man who ran the ferry. "You guys stay with the truck; I'll go down to the ferry. You got a can, in case I find a faucet that runs gas?"

Nobody laughed.

John climbed in the back of the truck and handed a jug out to Carlos, who then started down the hill.

Chapter Fifteen

Carlos swung the jug back and forth as he walked. He hoped he could finagle some gas out of the ferryman.

A truck came up the hill. John called, "Hey, Carlos, wait! He might stop."

Carlos turned around as the truck whizzed by him. John and Jerry stood in the middle of the road, waving their arms. This truck would have to stop, unless the driver wanted to run over the boys.

Carlos ran as the driver slammed on his brakes, stuck his head out and yelled, "What do you fool kids mean, standing in the middle of the road? You want to get killed? What's the idea?"

John said, "We're out of gas. Could you spare enough for us to get to camp?"

As John spoke, Carlos came up close to the back of the truck. He saw the canvas on the right side move, and then he saw two legs slip out from under it, followed by a body and arms, pushing the canvas aside. He stared in total disbelief. There stood Jo! She gave John's overalls a hitch and pulled a pillow from the truck.

"It's you!" Carlos cried. "Or else I'm seeing things!"

Just then the driver let out his clutch and yelled, "No, I haven't any extra gas. Get out of my way!"

John and Jerry turned around and gazed at Jo, their mouths hanging open. John yelled, "Straight from the sky. Jo! You're OK!"

Jerry grabbed one of her arms, and Carlos started pounding her back in his excitement. John pulled on Jerry. "Hey, leave her alone. You want to jerk her arms off?"

"Jo, how'd you get on that truck?" Jerry hollered as if she were a mile away.

"She hitched on, silly," John answered in a slightly calmer voice.

Carlos fell over a sage brush as he doubled up laughing. "She's a fruit tramp. She used her wits."

"Of course," John said. He sat down near Carlos. Jerry and Jo slumped down by them. Jo said, "I'm hungry and thirsty."

John got up and crawled into the seat of the truck and through the back curtain. He returned with a lemon drop, covered with lint. "Here, Jo, it was in my jacket pocket. There's nothing else to eat here."

"Come on, Jo. What happened? Did old Shorty grab you?" Carlos asked.

Jo pulled the lint from the lemon drop and popped it into her mouth. Then between exclamations, questions, and laughter, the boys heard the whole story.

Carlos reasoned, "I don't see what Shorty's game is."

"I know!" Jo said. "I didn't tell everything. It's money." She pulled the envelope out of her pocket and threw it on Carlos's lap. "I grabbed it when I got away. He wants your money."

Carlos pulled the letter out of the envelope. Tears

filled his eyes. He gulped. "It's the letter that tells about the interest my money made. It's money Mother and Father put in the bank for me when I was 3 days old. Mother said it wasn't much, but it would be when I'm of age, on account of the interest." He looked at his friends. "I always figured Shorty was dumb. He can't get this money. It's mine, and I can't have it till I'm 18. I suppose Shorty thought he'd take me to Sacramento and get his hands on it some way." He shoved the paper into his pocket. "So much for Shorty's scheme."

Jo glanced from one boy to the other. "You boys were sure nice to come looking for me. I didn't know how I'd get back to camp."

Jerry's habitual frown appeared. "We don't know how to get there either. We're out of gas. We won't get home before Dad, and that'll be trouble."

Carlos jumped up. "I was going to try the ferry! Remember?"

He grabbed the jug and said, "If anybody stops, you better say you're waiting for the guy you're with to get gas. That's the truth. Hide Jo if you see Shorty."

Jo said, "He'll probably be around. He'll want that letter."

Carlos started down the hill once again. His thoughts shifted. "The guy running the ferry must have gas. The thing to do is get a gallon of it." He hurried along, alert for pop bottles. He had picked up four by the time he got halfway to the bottom of the hill. "Worth eight cents," he muttered and hid them behind a bush until he came back.

Before the ferry started across, he walked up the ramp. The ferryman climbed down from his little house with a broom in his hand. He laughed. "Where'd you come from? I see you ran out of gas. No gas station—the only place to go is the ferry, huh?"

Carlos grinned. People liked a grin. "Yeah, no gas. We coasted some, but the car stopped at a level place. Do you have any gas?"

"Sure. I keep it on purpose for hard luckers. Here, give me your jug. While I'm gettin' your gas, sweep this trash into the river. I have a schedule to keep."

Carlos gave him the jug and grabbed the broom. He swept some bread scraps and popcorn to the ramp, and then into the river. He wondered to himself, *What should I do? I have no money to pay for the gas . . . Should I tell him I don't have any money, or grab the jug and run? No, of course, I'll never take off with the gas. That's out.*

The ferryman returned and took the broom. He handed Carlos the jug. "Here ya are, kid. Two bits is all I charge. You got the money, or is your dad paying when you cross?"

Carlos breathed deeply and let the air out, slow and easy. "I'll pay later."

He started back. He laughed out loud. "I got the gas. It's in the jug. I'll get two bits to him sometime, some-way, if I have to walk 50 miles. He trusted me, even if I am a fruit tramp."

Carlos wished he had something to eat. It seemed like it had been a long time since John had given him that oatmeal. Well, no use wishing.

He picked up the pop bottles, stuffing one in each hip pocket. He carried the other two under his left arm. His fingers cramped where he stuck them through the loop at the neck of the jug. "Hurt or no hurt, I better get along. What if Shorty happened to come by now? He must be sleeping beside the road somewhere, or maybe searching for Jo."

He glanced back at the ferry,chugging to the ramp on the other side. He bit his lip and frowned. An old Chevy drove onto the ramp. As he hurred on, he said into the air, "Be a good ferry, go slow. That old Chevy belongs to nobody but Shorty."

His chest ached and the bottles under his arm kept slipping. He sighed with relief when he saw the kids standing in the middle of the road, watching for him. He waved and beckoned. They came running.

"You've got it," John said matter-of-factly as he took the jug from Carlos.

"I'll take the pop bottles," Jerry offered. He grabbed the two from under Carlos's arm. Jo pulled the two out of his pockets.

"Take a look at the ferry," Carlos said.

"Shorty!" Jo exclaimed.

No one said a word the rest of the way to the truck.

John unscrewed the gas cap and poured the gas into the tank. "Climb in," John said. "Maybe we can get out of here before he sees us."

"Nope," Jerry said. "He's about on us."

John ordered, "Jo, you and Carlos get in the back and pull the curtain. He won't see you there."

Carlos followed Jo through the curtain. They sat hunched down on the edge of a bed.

John sat up tall as Shorty got out of his pickup and walked up to the car's window. "You kids from the park?" he asked.

Carlos watched Jerry ease out the door on his side while John answered Shorty. "Yeah, we're from the park. Do you live there?"

"No, I don't live there. You got that girl?"

"What girl?"

"You know what girl! She stole a valuable paper from me."

Carlos could see Jo's eyes in the semi-darkness. They were large and frightened. He grinned at her, even though he didn't feel like grinning. He put his finger to his lips, even though he couldn't hear her make a sound. He decided John was stalling. What good would it do?

John said, "We didn't bring a girl with us."

"Well, she lives by you. I mean to find her."

"Oh, you mean Jo. A lot of people are looking for her—my dad, her dad, and maybe the police by now."

"Don't be funny. Get out and open that back door so I can see."

John said, "Sorry, I can't do that. My dad gets mad if I wake him up."

Shorty paused a minute, looking undecided. "Another one of your lies, I suppose."

Carlos thought John was a good kid. He didn't lie; he just worked the words to suit the occasion.

"Oh, well," John said. "I'll open the back so you can see for yourself. Of course, anything might happen. This truck drives by itself. It might take off anytime. But come on; let's take a look."

Jo said, "That's a hint, Carlos! He wants you to drive off."

They crawled over the seat. Carlos pushed the

starter button, pumped on the gas, and pulled on the choke, but the engine didn't start.

Shorty bounded around to the front, his face red and angry looking. "You!" he sputtered. "I knew you were here." He made a frantic grab for the door handle and pulled on it just as the motor started. Carlos turned the wheel sharply to the left to avoid Shorty's car and tramped on the gas, jerking the door handle from Shorty's grasp. He finished the turn out in the sage brush and careened back on the road, heading toward camp.

Jo stuck her head out the window to report, "Shorty's shaking his fist! . . . John and Jerry are running this way . . . Now Shorty's getting in his car—no, he's getting out. He's looking at his tires."

Carlos gripped the wheel tight. Boy, if he ever got this truck back to camp, he'd be glad.

Jo kept reporting. "Shorty's not following us, and the boys are still running. Maybe we should back up for them."

"Back up!" Carlos exclaimed. "That's what I hate to do." He pulled over to the side of the road and got out. Sure enough, Shorty hadn't moved his pickup. He was working a tire pump up and down. Carlos laughed. That Jerry had slipped around and let the air out of Shorty's tires.

Carlos got behind the wheel again and backed up, staying in the middle of the road—most of the time. Sometimes he swerved from side to side. When he reached John and Jerry, they piled in quickly and Carlos started off.

John said, "To camp, Carlos! He'll be on the road again soon."

Chapter Sixteen

Carlos didn't take his eyes off the road. He asked, "What's going on? Is Shorty still pumping his tire?"

Jo pulled the curtain back. "No, he's getting into his car."

John directed, "Carlos, see those cottonwood trees ahead, along the curve? Drive in between and behind them—there's enough space. He can't see us there, and he'll drive by."

"Maybe," Jerry retorted.

Jo watched anxiously as Carlos drove in among the trees and waited for the old Chevy to go by.

Carlos said, "He's got it floor-boarded."

Jo glimpsed the flash of an angry face as Shorty raced by. How mean he looked!

Carlos pulled onto the road again. They kept quiet as the truck rattled along. Jo wondered how much farther it was to camp. They hadn't gone by the gas station, but it must be close.

Jerry complained, "We'll probably run out of gas again before we get back to camp."

They all groaned.

John said, "Good ol' doomsday man had to put it in words! But I must say that I've been worryin' some myself."

Jo started twisting her hair. "How far will we get?" she asked.

"Not quite there, I'm afraid," John muttered.

Jerry added, "I knew we'd never make it."

Jo thought to herself. "We *have* to make it. No one knows where we are. Only God; He knows everything. Please help us, God! We have to get gas."

"How about the little store with the gas pump?" she asked.

John shrugged. "No money."

"The pop bottles!" Jo exclaimed.

"Great," Jerry said. "Only that won't even get us eight drops of gas."

John frowned. "Be still, Jerry. Look around in back. See if you can find more bottles."

They scrambled around in the back and looked under the bed, in the corners, and under piles of the boys' pants.

"I found one!" Jo exclaimed triumphantly.

Jerry yelled, "Here's a big one!"

Jo took a deep breath as they continued on down the road. That made five bottles, plus a big one. She felt sure they could make it now. She leaned over the seat and watched Carlos reach with his foot to touch the gas pedal. Then his foot relaxed some, and the truck slowed down.

Jerry yelled, "We're out of gas!"

"Not yet," John said quietly. "Carlos is resting his foot a minute."

Jo's stomach felt cramped with hunger and worry at the thought of Mom and Dad getting home before they did. They hadn't missed her last night, but they would now. Daddy might hunt, but he'd never find them, even if he looked all night.

After traveling a few more miles they arrived at the little store. Carlos stopped by the pump. No one came out to wait on them.

"Probably closed," Jerry remarked. "Shorty's going to turn around. Then what'll we do?"

No one bothered to answer. John and Carlos gathered up the bottles, and they all trooped into the store. An old man with a long white beard nodded at them. "Howdy."

John said, "We want to trade these bottles for gas." They set the bottles on the counter and the old man counted them.

Jo started twisting her hair again. It seemed to take the old man a long time. Surely he'd give them gas.

The storekeeper asked, "Do you have a car with a house affair on the back?"

Jo's heart skipped a beat. How did he know about the little house?

John answered, "Sure thing. When we travel, some of us can even sleep."

The old man followed them out to the truck. He took the gas hose down and looked at them, then he unscrewed the gas cap and looked again.

Jo watched Carlos tighten his fists every time the man hesitated. The man looked again, put the hose in the tank, pulled on his whiskers, and bent his head forward. "Was that your dad who stopped here, looking for kids in a truck?"

Carlos stalled. "Did the guy drive an old Chevy?"

"Yeah."

John shrugged. "He's from down by the camp. He doesn't have any kids."

Picking up the story, Jo added, "There's something wrong with him. He tried to make out I was his daughter. I mean, his son."

Carlos laughed. "Yeah, and that he's my father. Anybody can tell that's not true."

Jo laughed a little. It helped for Carlos to be Mexican.

The old man smiled broadly. "He probably always wanted kids of his own. Wait a minute." He went inside and reappeared with four huge cookies. "My wife baked today. Here's one for each of you."

They took the cookies, thanked him, and climbed into the truck. Jo stuck her head out the window. "These are good cookies. We can't bake on a camp stove. Thank you."

They started out again, eating their cookies on the way.

Jerry remarked, "These cookies sure drop to the bottom. I'm plum hollow."

The others laughed in agreement.

They hadn't gone far when they spied the old Chevy coming toward them. Shorty swerved his car close to them as he passed. Carlos gripped the wheel and held to the road.

Jo leaned over and stuck her head out the window. She yelled, "He's turning around. Hurry up, Carlos!"

Jerry cried, "He's right behind us!"

Shorty honked his horn, and then bore down on it, not letting up.

"He wants you to stop," Jo exclaimed.

"Let him want," John said.

"He's going to bump us!" Jerry cried out.

They felt a jar from the rear, and then another. Carlos gripped the wheel harder and sped up a little. Shorty drove up beside them and yelled, "Pull over!"

"Don't do it," John fumed. "He can't make you."

Carlos said, "He'll ram us, sideswipe us, or anything to get what he wants."

"I said, pull over!" Shorty yelled again.

Carlos said quietly, "I better go with him. He's going to wreck us."

Jo encouraged, "Just keep going, Carlos. We'll make it. We have to."

"Pull over!"

They approached a curve. Jo looked at a wall of high rocks. There was a steep incline from the side of the road to the bottom of the rocks. She said, "I hope nobody's coming around that corner."

At that moment, a long black car appeared.

"Here goes!" Carlos yelled.

Shorty swerved toward the shoulder, but the black car sideswiped the old Chevy with a terrific impact. The Chevy hit loose gravel and rolled over the incline between the rocks and the road.

Carlos drove the truck to the side of the road and stopped. He was the first one to run toward the wrecked Chevy. The others followed close behind. They slowed to a walk as they came closer to the wreck.

Carlos said, "I should have pulled over, like Shorty told me to, then this wouldn't have happened. Shorty's mean, but I didn't want to hurt him."

They came to a halt by the men from the black car.

They all stood gazing down at the old Chevy. It was up-side down, and the doors hung open. Shorty legs were slung around the steering column, and his shoulders and head hung down in the top of the car.

Jo put her hands down deep into her big pockets and grasped the material in her clammy hands.

"He's awful quiet," John said.

As if trying to deny the truth, Jo pointed to his fore-head. "But there isn't any blood—only that little spurt from up in his hair."

The driver of the black car spoke to his companion. "There doesn't have to be a wreck with both cars jammed up and a lot of blood loss to cause serious consequences. His neck might be broken."

The other man replied, "You're right, doctor." Together they stepped down beside the wrecked car.

Carlos leaned closer and gazed at Shorty as if he couldn't look away. He sighed and stepped back when John gave him a slight pull.

The men carefully untangled Shorty's legs from the steering column and lifted him onto a level place. The doctor pressed with his finger under Shorty's right ear.

Jerry whispered hoarsely, "What's he doin'?"

John said, "He's seein' if his heart's beatin'."

The doctor shook his head, and the other man handed him a black bag from the car.

John said quietly, "He's sure enough a doctor."

The doctor took a mirror from the bag and held it above Shorty's mouth, and then in front of his nostrils. He stood and shook his head sadly. "Not much breath. I'm sorry to say, he's bad off. I'll cross on the ferry, report the accident, and send an ambulance. I don't believe it will take long. Do you mind staying here until I come back?" he asked his friend.

"Of course, someone must stay. It's fortunate your car only received a few dents. Why anyone would try to pass on a curve like this is beyond me."

The doctor stepped back beside Jo and the others. "Thank you for stopping. No need for you to linger."

The children walked slowly back to the truck. Jo glanced at Carlos. She knew he wasn't glad about what had happened.

Jerry said, "Well, we don't have to worry about Shorty for a while."

John grabbed his brother's arm and shook him. "Don't ever say anything like that again. It didn't need to turn out this way, and we're sorry. Do you hear?"

"OK," Jerry said quietly.

Carlos looked back. "All the time I hated him; now it's like you said, Jo, I'm sorry for him."

Tears rolled down Jo's face and she couldn't stop them. Soon she was sobbing and shaking all over.

Carlos pulled on her arm. "Don't cry, Jo."

John awkwardly patted her on the shoulder. "Come on, Jo, we gotta get back to camp."

With the boys encouraging her, Jo straightened up and climbed into the truck with them. They drove along quietly for a long time. At last Jerry broke the silence. "Mom and Dad'll probably be in camp. Wait and see."

"Good ol' Jerry, bring up more trouble." His brother sighed.

Carlos groaned. "Me driving into camp with your

dad there."

"And my folks," Jo added.

John consoled them. "Dort'll tell them what happened. I don't think they'll be mad."

"They'll be searching for us," Jerry grumbled. "Dad always says to be in camp when they get back from work."

No one had a solution to the problem. Carlos drove very carefully. After some time, he said, "Shorty didn't want me around. He wanted my money. Now he's hurt, hurt bad. And I might have killed us all. I should have gone with him. I've brought all kinds of trouble."

As they approached camp Jo pointed. "There's the gas station and the old people on the seats, waiting for customers . . . There's people coming home from swimming over the bridge."

As Carlos drove cautiously down the camp road, Jerry said, "And there's old busybody out there in front of our camp with all of our folks—even Dort's dad. She's wavin' her arms and goin' on as usual."

John said, "Who cares? We're back."

Carlos swerved in by John's camp, barely missing the tent ropes. The truck sputtered, and the motor died all by itself. Carlos said, "Out of gas again."

They could hear the woman with the tied-up boys carrying on. "There they are! See? He's drivin' your truck, just like I said. They run around foolin' here and there all day long, that gang!"

Jo covered her ears with her hands and whispered, "You did it, God. We're back. Thank You!"

Chapter Seventeen

ohn's father took a deep breath as he looked at the upset woman. Then in a firm voice he said, "OK, OK. We'll take care of the situation, lady. Don't you worry about it anymore."

Carlos slid down in the seat and John jumped out. He said, "Dort, why didn't you explain?"

Dort's voice quivered. "I tried to, but she talked all the time. I couldn't get a word in edgewise."

Jo's mother looked in the truck. "Where's Jo?"

Jo slid over the seat and slipped outside. "I'm here, Mom."

Jo's father took hold of her arm with a strong grip. "Young lady, you have some explaining to do."

John's father said, "Hold it, Bruce. John wouldn't do this unless he had a good reason. I know my kid. Let's listen."

Dort took Jo's hand while John explained the whole thing, with Jo and Jerry offering additions here and there.

Jo's mother put her arm around Jo and hugged her. Daddy pulled her to him and gave her a little swat to show how glad he was to have her safe. Jo saw Carlos slide even farther down in the seat. Why didn't he get out?

Later, Jo opened the truck door. "Come on, Carlos. We're having supper. Mom said to have you eat with us." She wondered if he was afraid and added, "Don't worry.

We told the folks everything—even about your hideaway and about Shorty. Come on!"

At supper Carlos acted quiet and shy. Jo couldn't believe her ears when he refused seconds. He finished eating and thanked them for the meal, then he slipped around to his hideaway. Why had he left so soon? It wouldn't be dark for a long time. "He's probably thinking about Shorty," Jo decided. "He was Carlos's stepfather, even if he was a mean man."

When Daddy went over to Dort's camp after supper, Jo followed, still thinking about how Shorty had bothered Carlos. Carlos *had* to hide from him. She wanted Shorty to be all right, but she hoped he stayed away from Carlos.

The men talked about their jobs and about getting another one. Jo heard Daddy say, "I guess most of the orchards will finish up this week. The hops are about ready."

Dort pulled on Jo's arm. "Did you know you're going to the same hop yard we are? It's the same place we picked last year."

Jo clasped Dort's hands. Whirling around together, the girls fell in a giggling heap. When they settled down, Dort said, "Mama's getting her operation tomorrow. The doctor said she would come out of it OK. Your dad's going to save us a camping spot by your family in the hop camp."

Jo said, "Oh, good!"

"Mama and the baby will go to Grandma's in town, when they get out of the hospital. Tiny and I'll go with Dad to pick hops."

Jo squeezed Dort's hand. "I'm glad your mama's going to be all right."

Dort glanced down at their clasped hands. "Hey,

you're unbuttoned." She reached for Jo's cuff. "I'll button it."

Jo said, "That's OK; let it go."

But Dort had already seen Jo's arm. "Your marks aren't near as dark as mine," she said. "Hey, you lost the button."

Jo skipped the lost button remark and asked, "Where is your birthmark?"

"Didn't you ever notice it?" She leaned her head back so her long dark hair hung away from her neck. A reddish-brown spot ran between her ear and shoulder on the right side.

Jo gazed at the spot until Dort straightened her head up. She thought, *Dort doesn't care if I see that. It's just Dort. These things on my arm are just Jo.* She rolled both sleeves up.

The girls followed their fathers to John's camp to talk to John's dad. The three men continued their conversation about the hops.

"Slim, we're going to a good place to pick—a clean camp ground for pickers. They give you a sack of spuds when you register and sell milk for half-price. Nice people. You know how it is in hops. If you get there early enough, you have a job. There's no trouble about that. You better come with us."

Slim agreed with Dort's father. "Sounds good to me. We'll tag along."

John and Jo grinned at each other. Jo thought, "All my friends willl be together."

Mom called to Jo. "You better tie up Mitsy. There are several campers moving out this evening. She's liable to go along."

Jo called Mitsy, but she didn't come. Dort and Tiny

went with her up the camp road. "Mitsy; come, Mitsy!" they called. But they couldn't find her anywhere.

Jo said, "Mitsy is probably home by now. I know she wouldn't go with anyone."

They circled back, still calling and peering here and there for the little white dog.

John yelled, "Maybe she's out with Carlos."

Jo said, "Mitsy would come if she heard us. She's not out there."

Mom was worried. "If someone didn't take her she's probably gone up on the road. She'll get run over by a car."

"Don't worry, Mom, we'll find her," Daddy consoled. "There isn't much traffic."

Jo held Daddy's hand, and they walked to the road and across the bridge. Soon John and Mom came running behind them, out of breath.

"Carlos is gone; his outfit and everything!" John panted.

Just then Mitsy came around the bend with Carlos right behind her. His bedroll flopped back and forth on his back as he threw rocks at Mitsy and yelled, "Go on back to camp. You can't go with me. Go! Go!" He threw another rock at the dog.

When Carlos saw them, he stopped.

John exclaimed, "That's what I meant—Carlos moved on! Your mom and I went out to his hideaway."

Mitsy ran into Jo's arms, and Carlos walked toward them. He stopped in front of Jo and said, "I've been trying to make Mitsy go back to your camp. I chased her, threw stones, and yelled."

Daddy lifted the bedroll off Carlos's back. "Where are you going with this heavy load, son?"

"Just goin'."

Daddy nodded. "Well, we're going to the hops to-morrow, and you might as well come along."

Jo hugged Mitsy close in her arms. Would Carlos agree? Sometimes he could be stubborn if he got an idea into his head. She thought he looked as though he couldn't believe Daddy.

He asked, "What do you mean?"

Daddy put his hand on Carlos's shoulder. "We'd like to have you travel with us."

Carlos frowned. "It costs money to have an extra mouth to feed. I know that."

"You can help in different ways. Only one thing: I'm head of the family. If you get tired of me being boss, talk it over with me. Don't sneak off."

Carlos smiled and Daddy held out his hand, and they shook on the arrangement. Carlos promised, "When I'm older, I can help you more."

"That's a deal," Daddy said.

Carlos asked Mom, "Is it OK with you?"

"It was my idea first," she said.

Carlos looked sad. "I wonder if you know the accident was my fault. If I'd pulled the truck over like Shorty told me, to it wouldn't have happened. I should have stopped. It's my fault he's hurt."

Jo interrupted, "No, Carlos; you wanted to stop. We told you not to. We're all to blame."

"That's right," John added.

They walked back on the bridge. Jo leaned on the railing and watched the river flow past as they talked. She hoped everything would turn out happy, like in a book.

126

Daddy said, "Carlos, Shorty left you all alone. He abandoned you. After that I don't see how you'd be obligated to mind him when he ordered you to stop. Besides, he failed to be a careful driver. He was definitely in the wrong. I could have had him jailed for kidnapping Jo, for leaving you, and for driving like a madman. Of course you're sorry it happened. We all are. But you're not to blame. The other children are not to blame either. Shorty acted foolish. He punished himself. He got caught in his own trap."

Jo smiled. Daddy always made things right. Of course Carlos couldn't be to blame anymore than the rest of them. Even so, Shorty was gone, and he had nobody to care.

Daddy looked at Carlos kindly. "After we get located in the hops, we'll find out what happened to Shorty and where he is."

She watched the expression on Carlos's face turn to relief. He grinned at Jo, took his bedroll from Daddy, and they all started to camp.

Carlos said, "I'm a fast hop picker. I can pick faster than a lot of big folks."

Daddy laughed. "I'll hold you to that." He added, "Remember, Carlos, you're part of the family."

Mom said, "We need a boy in the family."

Jo grabbed Carlos's hand. "It's like we're brother and sister."

Carlos smiled the biggest smile Jo had ever seen.

She laughed. "I've got a brother!"

They broke camp two days later. Carlos made himself available every time someone was needed to help.

They moved to the hops and saved a spot next to theirs for Dort's family. The boys' family made camp facing the camp road, straight across from Dort's space. After getting settled, they went to Yakima for groceries.

They drove into camp late. Jo saw an old car parked across the narrow gravel road from the owner's house. It looked like Shorty's Chevy, but of course she knew it couldn't be.

Chapter Eighteen

The next morning Jo remembered seeing the car that had reminded her of Shorty's. It couldn't have been his, of course, because he had banged up his old Chevy in the accident, and the doctor had said Shorty's neck might be broken.

She slipped quickly into a pair of jeans and one of her long-sleeved shirts. She noticed that the sleeves were getting short on her and that some of the spots showed. "I'm growing, and the spots are getting lighter. They aren't important anymore," she decided.

She walked by their car, where Carlos slept in the back seat. She looked at him, all stretched out, and laughed. "Grandma would say 'Your covers are all skeejawed.'"

When she got to the boss man's house, she peered around the corner. The old car was still there. It did look like Shorty's car—even to a bent back fender.

"It can't be! I want to look at the driver's side." She slipped across the road, behind the car, and peeked around the left back fender. She gasped. The car had no front fender! The door dangled and swayed at a slight movement in the front seat. Wire was all that held the door on.

Can it be Shorty's car? she asked herself. She crept closer. Inside, a man slept with his head lolled over the back of the seat. His hands had slid from the steering wheel. His red face and red hair blended together in one bright blob.

Jo felt goose bumps forming on her arms. This man and Shorty had been together when they left Carlos off by her camp. Where was Shorty? How did old Red get Shorty's car? How could the engine run after being wrecked?

She hurried back to her camp. Carlos was sitting up in the car, his mouth open wide in a big yawn.

"Carlos! Carlos! Shorty's car is out front." Quickly, she told him what she had discovered. "How could he get the Chev to run?" she asked.

"Old Red is good with motors. He can make anything with four wheels go. He never fixes rattles or anything that's falling apart, but he puts a little bailing wire here and there to make everything hang together." He frowned. "I don't understand how he got Shorty's car."

"Come on, Carlos. Let's find out." They circled the camp, skirting around a tall building. "That's a hop kiln. They dry the hops after they're picked," Carlos explained.

Jo shrugged. "Let's find out about Shorty. Do you suppose he died?"

"Shorty's mean, but I hope he got along all right," Carlos murmured. They went by the house. The old car was still there.

Carlos grumbled, "Red can sleep all night and all day. Jo, he's by himself. He won't touch me. In fact, he got after Shorty for knockin' me around. I'm going to find out what's what. They approached the car as Red climbed over the wired-up door.

"Hello there, Carlos. I've been looking for you. That woman with the men babies told me you left with this girl's folks. I recognized their camp."

"Where'd you get Shorty's Chev?"

"Shorty's all banged up. He's laid up in the Toppenish Hospital. This chiropractor doctor took him there. I was getting' out when he came in. I had an attack, and somebody took me there. Shorty told me where they'd put his car, so I got it."

Carlos frowned. "What do you want?"

"Shorty told me to get you. Grab your stuff and come on."

Carlos laughed. "Tell Shorty I'm through with him like he was through with me when he dumped me in camp."

"You holdin' that against him?"

"Hardly. He did me a favor. I'm going to travel with Jo's folks now."

"Maybe so, Carlos, but Shorty said you're not a citizen here, and if you don't come with me, when he gets out of the hospital, he'll dump you in Mexico."

"That's some of Shorty's blowin'."

Red climbed back over the wired-up door. "I'm going to the hospital now. I'll tell Shorty what you said. You could camp with me until he gets out, you know." He started the old car and rattled away.

"Can Shorty take you to Mexico?"

"I'm a citizen of the United States. I was born in Texas. I have my birth certificate, that paper from the bank, and a picture of my mother, father, and me when I was 1 year old. I'll show it all to you. Come on."

They returned to camp and climbed into the back seat

of the car. Carlos rummaged in his things and brought out the leather envelope. He frowned. "You know, once Shorty gets an idea, nobody can change it. He thinks he can get my money that's in the bank, no matter what. If he thinks he can take me to Mexico and leave me, no one can make him think differently. I can't, because he believes I lie."

"But you can prove where you were born by your birth certificate. He can't do anything, can he?"

"He can try. If he tried, it would cause trouble, and proving things is done by a lawyer. Lawyers cost money."

"What will you do?"

"Sit tight. Wait and see what he tries. Funny thing, Jo, I've never been to Mexico. Someday I'll take a trip there."

He pulled a rubber band from around the leather envelope and brought out some papers. He handed one to Jo. She read: Carlos Jesus Garcia, born in El Paso, Texas. His father's name was the same as his, and his mother's name was Marie Angel Garcia.

He handed her a black and white snapshot, rumpled at the edges. Jo noticed the woman had on a flowered dress and the man wore a white shirt. They were both smiling at Carlos, who had on a striped suit. She thought, *They're proud of him.*

She handed the picture back. "Keep it always, Carlos. Mom has a trunk she keeps things in. She would take care of your important papers for you."

"I'll ask her later," Carlos said, returning everything to the envelope and snapping the rubber band around it. He sighed. "Mother said Shorty was thick. She meant he couldn't understand anything. He probably doesn't know there's a record of my birth in Texas. He might figure all he has to do is destroy my birth certificate, and then threaten me. I guess he thinks Mexicans have to live in Mexico.

As they got out of the car John and his brothers ran over. John slapped Carlos on the shoulder. "We're all here. I'm sure glad you're with Jo's folks now."

Carlos smiled from ear to ear and then grew serious as he told them about Red.

"Oh, phooey!" John exclaimed.

Jo heard voices from a tent that hadn't been next to hers that morning. She ran toward the tent yelling, "Dort; Tiny!" The girls grabbed hands, giggled, and all talked at once. Finally Jo asked, "How's your mother?"

"She's all right. The operation was this morning. Daddy's going back to Mama this afternoon. Tomorrow he'll be here to start picking. Grandma will take the baby and care for it until Mama gets out of the hospital. They will stay with Grandma until the hops are picked."

"I'm glad everything's going to be all right, like the Bible lady said, if you talk to God about it."

"Yes," Dort and Tiny said together.

"I have to help unpack dishes and other things. Daddy's going to leave right after breakfast to see Mama. Tiny and I will stay with you."

"Oh, goody! See you then."

Mom called, "Jo, you and Carlos get washed for breakfast and fill the water pails. The faucet is around the corner of that little red building."

While Jo had her face in the water, Carlos grabbed the buckets and headed for the faucet, soon to return with them full.

133

"No, Carlos, don't you start spoiling Jo. She has to help. Two buckets, two kids."

Carlos grinned, "Whatever you say."

Jo had been taught never to bring up problems at a meal—besides, she was hungry—so she didn't mention Shorty's old car. Carlos didn't either.

When Mom worked, she had no time to make pancakes. But this morning they had pancakes smeared with butter and syrup.

Carlos rubbed his tummy. "Thanks for the larapin cakes."

Daddy smiled. "We have a boy with manners."

Mom patted Carlos on the head. "You're welcome. Now you kids run along and explore. Daddy and I have some business to discuss, and mail to look over. And maybe we'll read the paper we got last night."

Jo grabbed Carlos's arm. "Come on!"

They walked by the hop kiln and across the end of one of the hop yards. She gazed at the vines stretching from the ground to the wires. She said, "The wires are high, maybe twice as high as our tent."

"Yes, about 15 feet high."

"Carlos, do they use ladders to pick the hops?"

"No. Each picker has a long pole with a curved knife on the end. He cuts a vine down and, if it's hot, drags it under the shade of the next vine to pick into a big basket. Then it's dumped into a sack to be weighed."

They walked between two rows. Jo wrinkled her nose. "They smell strange."

"It's supposed to be a healthy smell. Some people put hops in a pillowcase and sleep on it."

A few hops grew on the bottom of the vines. Jo pulled one off that was about two inches long. It was fluffy. She rubbed it between her fingers. The yellow pollen and little green leaves looked pretty. She stuck part of it in her mouth. "Eeek," she screamed immediately, and spewed it out. "It's bitter."

"They're not to eat. They make beer and stuff out of them."

Next, they walked out of the hop yard. "It looks like green waves. Each row is a wave," Jo said.

Carlos glanced toward camp. "Hey, there's the boys." They ran and joined them under a small tree.

Soon Dort and Tiny's father drove out of camp and the girls came over too. They all sat down on the ground and discussed Shorty's threat to dump Carlos in Mexico.

"I thought you were through with him," Jerry grumbled.

Jim and Tiny muttered together, "Yeah."

"He can't do anything but be a bother," John stated.

"Maybe," Carlos added.

Jo worried to herself. John says he's a bother. Carlos says he'll sit tight and see. But, I might lose my brother."

Chapter Nineteen

Daddy bounded out of the tent, a newspaper fluttering in his hand. "Hey, Slim, are you going to the parade in Toppenish today?"

John's father met Daddy between the camps and the two looked over the newspaper.

Slim said, "My gang would jump at the chance, and my wife wants to go. Sure, we'll go."

"Let's meet in front of the courthouse and go together. We better start early. Parades get crowded."

The arrangements were made. Carlos put his bedroll in the tent, but Jo noticed he shoved his leather envelope under the front seat. *He shouldn't do that. It might get lost,* she thought.

Mitsy whined when Mom tied her to the leg of the bed. Mom patted her. "You can't go, Mitsy. You might get lost, and it's too hot for a little dog."

Dort, Tiny, Jo, and Carlos sat in the back seat. When Daddy started, Jo thought, *We are like a big family with four kids. That would be nice, but I have a brother and that's enough.* She remembered how it had taken a whole loaf of bread to make sandwiches for all of the kids. Large families needed more money.

When both families had parked, Daddy said, "You

kids know where the car is. If we get separated, meet here after the parade. Stay together."

John's father gave the boys money for ice cream. Daddy gave Jo and the girls money too, but Carlos objected when he came to him.

"Are you my hijo?"

"Yes."

"Then have ice cream."

Carlos grinned. "Sure."

Jo thought the parade was wonderful. The float the Indian princess rode on had little trees and cedar boughs for a background. The princess wore a dress of buckskin that was almost white. It had beads on it, and fringes on the bottom and the sleeves. Her headband and moccasins were also beaded.

Dort took a deep breath. "She's so pretty. Look at her beautiful long braids."

The boys especially liked the float on which six young Indian men rode. Their bodies were covered with grease, and they had nothing on except a breechcloth and headband. They danced around in a circle, tomahawks raised menacingly at each other.

Toward the end of the parade, when it seemed to be nothing but officials riding in their cars, Jo whispered to Carlos, "I have an idea."

"What?"

"You ought to visit Shorty and tell him his stunt won't work, that you have a birth certificate." She laughed. "And give him the paper from the bank. You could explain about the paper."

"He wouldn't believe me."

"Let him take the paper to the California bank and find out you don't lie."

Carlos frowned. "I guess he can't do anything to me when he's all banged up in bed. My envelope's with the papers in the car."

"We can tell our parents we found Shorty ourselves," Jo planned.

As they were slipping away, Jo heard Slim say, "I guess that money's burning a hole in the kids' pockets. They're going to hunt up ice cream."

They went to the car, and Carlos pulled his leather envelope from under the seat.

"Now we must find the hospital," Jo said. After inquiring from a storekeeper and three people on the street, they found the hospital.

"Carlos, you better not get too close to Shorty with your papers. He's liable to grab them and call for the nurse when you try to get them back. Probably say you are bothering him," John advised.

"You're right."

Carlos and Jo stepped inside, and their friends sat on the steps to wait for them. Carlos hesitated, but Jo went straight to a counter with an information sign. Suddenly she realized he wouldn't be registered as Shorty. She turned to Carlos and whispered, "What's his real name?"

"William Brown."

The lady gave Carlos and then Jo a stern look. "Only his friend is allowed to see him."

Carlos said, "I'm his stepson."

Jo added, "I'm not a relative. I'll stay in the hall outside his room."

"He's in room 203, but no children." She pointed to an area with a couch. "You can wait there for your mother." She turned from them and started rearranging stuffed animals in the gift store.

Jo grabbed Carlos by the hand, and they walked down the hall and stopped by some stairs. "She isn't very sharp. Did she think our mother stood by us?"

"I guess so," Carlos replied.

Jo noticed tears rolling down Carlos's cheeks. She started to ask him what was the matter, but stopped when Carlos reared back his shoulders and set his jaw firmly. "This hospital is much smaller than the one my mother died in."

Jo gave him a slight pull, and they headed up the stairs. "We are breaking a hospital rule, but your mother would want you to settle with Shorty."

"Yes, and she would be happy I'm with your folks."

When they got to the top of the stairs, Jo pointed to a room with "203" in large numbers at the top of the door.

A nurse stepped into a room, then out again, and pushed the door open to another room, calling, "See you tomorrow, Eddie."

They dodged into a little room where linen was stored. Jo's heart felt like it was fluttering around in her throat. She squeezed Carlos's hand.

"We're this far; we might as well try to finish the job," he muttered low in his throat.

"I guess so," Jo agreed.

"I think she's made her rounds and is headed somewhere else. That's the way they do. Let's go."

They dashed to room 203. Carlos stepped inside, near Shorty's bed. Jo stood by the door, out of sight from the hall.

Shorty's neck was in a big brace, and his left arm had a heavy cast on it. He looked uncomfortable as he shifted his legs while never moving the upper part of his body.

"Decided to come after all, eh? Well, as you can see, I'm not going anywhere for a while. What happened? I suppose that girl's folks kicked you out. You decided it might get cold with winter coming. California sounds pretty good. Red told me what you said."

When he paused for a breath, Carlos said, "I've been worried about you. I didn't know where you were."

Shorty snorted, "I bet. You wanted help, that's all."

"No, I don't need help. I want to show you a couple papers." He took the papers from his leather envelope and held the birth certificate in front of Shorty, who squinted at it.

Then Carlos flashed the other paper before him. "This is the letter from the bank you wanted. I can't get that money until I'm 18 years old. You can't get it either—with me or without me."

A man in a bathrobe came into the room and headed for the other bed. "Not a nurse around," he laughed. "They probably took off to the parade."

No one answered him. Shorty glared at Carlos. "You know I can't read much. You know I'm not good at figures. Everybody can't go to school. You're tryin' to pull a shenanigan on me. You're lying!"

Jo touched Shorty's roommate on the arm. "Would you please read Carlos's papers to Shorty?"

The man came closer and took the papers Carlos handed him. "Sure. Anything to please a pretty little girl." The birth certificate was on top. He read every word and every number on the whole page. "This young fellow must be Carlos Jesus Garcia. You have a lot to live up to with a name like that."

Shorty's face bulged out as he silently fumed.

The man put the birth certificate under the bank paper. No one said anything as he read the paper. "Shorty, it looks as if your friend here has money in the bank drawing interest. When he's 18, he can take it out."

Shorty continued to glare as the man said, "It's a good thing you can't get it before you're 18—you'd just spend it! What you should do is send a little money to that bank in California whenever you can. Then you can go to college later, or go into business."

Carlos smiled. "That sounds like a good idea. Maybe I'll go into business with Bruce."

Jo thanked the man as he handed the papers back and sat down on the side of his bed. She came closer to Shorty's bed. "I want you to know that all of us are sorry the accident happened. None of us wanted you hurt, especially Carlos."

Ignoring her, Shorty glared at Carlos, fiercer than ever. His face almost purple, he sputtered, "So that's that! Get out of here. I'm not taking you anywhere with me. I don't want to lay my eyes on you again."

"Suits me," Carlos whispered to himself as they went out the door.

A nurse appeared from one of the rooms. She put her hand on Jo's shoulder. "Didn't anyone downstairs tell you children are not allowed to visit patients?"

"We're leaving," Jo said.

They hurried outside and told the others about the visit.

John shrugged. "We were sorry about the accident, but nobody wants to see him again."

On the way to the car they stopped and got their ice cream. No one talked much, they just licked their cones and thought about what had happened.

Jo said, "The Bible lady explained many things to us. I'm glad I can talk to God when I have problems. He's taken care of us."

John added, "Me, too."

"He really loves us," Carlos agreed. "And we are His children."

The parents were waiting for them. Daddy gave Jo a puzzled look.

Carlos looked first at Mom, then at Daddy. "Maybe we should have told you what we were up to. You said you'd find out what happened to Shorty. Well, we found out." With Jo's help and a word or two from John, Carlos told about Shorty's Chevy and Red and the hospital visit.

Daddy slapped Carlos on the back. "Good work, hijo. I won't have to keep my promise about finding Shorty. You have taken care of everything yourself."

"The hospital visit was Jo's idea," Carlos said.

Mom's knowing look appeared. "I can imagine. Jo's full of ideas."

Slim walked toward the driver's side of their truck. "I think that guy's hash is pretty well settled."

The girls and Carlos climbed into the back seat, and Mom sat close to Daddy in the front. Mom started singing a funny little ditty about a curly black bug. Of course that started all of them singing funny songs and old favorites, even Daddy.

As they drove into camp, they were singing "Home Sweet Home."